TOUCH YOUR NOSE

MATTHEW LEDREW

TOUCH YOUR NOSE
THE ENGEN UNIVERSE

Published in Canada by Engen Books, St. John's, NL.

Library and Archives Canada Cataloguing in Publication

LeDrew, Matthew, 1984-, author
    Touch your nose / Matthew LeDrew.

ISBN 978-1-926903-78-1 (softcover)

    I. Title.

PS8623.E424T68 2018   C813'.6   C2018-902614-6

Distributed by:
Engen Books
www.engenbooks.com
submissions@engenbooks.com

First mass market paperback printing: May 2018

Cover Image: Drop Dead Designs

For
Ellen

CHAPTER ONE

I was eighteen months deep cover when I finally got my first real in. Not deep cover as in fake mustache either, but real deep cover. No–friends–no–family–don't–forget–to–talk–with–your–American–accent deep cover. Eighteen months.

The first seven months were spent managing a failing restaurant in Virginia, a place so bad they did a two-episode stint of Kitchen Nightmares on it. After that started turning a major profit, there were three months as a management consultant – three months is not a long time to build a reputation though, so it was something of a smash-and-grab, a lot of dollars spent to get my reputation to where it needed to be. By my ninth month of deep cover, I was turning down interviews for Forbes. That got me the attention of head hunters, and then it was just a matter of waiting for the right offer. It took me a month to get a call from Tyler Carter, VP of the San Diego Valley division of Shane Enterprises. I'd been there eight months when I'd gotten my opening.

Eighteen months, and the accent was only just starting to feel natural in my mouth.

My name is Simon Monk, and this is what I do.

It was at an office Christmas party, which was being held in mid-November. December was a busy month for us; everything needed to be filed and catalogued and pressed and stamped and put into boxes, or so I was told – it was my first Christmas on the job. So Christmas got pushed ahead to November. Christmas in San Diego – in any month really – is an oxymoron. I spent any time I wasn't at the office going commando in shorts and standing in front of my AC for hours on end reading *Businessman Weekly*. At the party I was wearing a suit and tie – most were here for fun, but I was here to work. It was actually the first time I'd really been working in eighteen months.

Tyler had rented the penthouse suite of the convention center for the night. The room was huge and dark with Maplewood floors, three bars, and a glass ceiling that looked out over the whole city and up to a blanket of deep blue full of stars above. It was enough to make anyone feel romantic.

There was a patio that stretched all the way around the floor and looked out upon a view that dropped thirty stories to the street below. It was vertigo inducing. The patio was filled with smokers trying to escape the cool air-conditioned and clean-smelling interior of the penthouse for the stale swarmy smoke of their cigarettes. I wanted to be smoking. I'd quit eighteen months ago. Smokers are off-putting to non-smokers, but non-smokers appeal to everyone. This wasn't Mad Men and I wasn't Jon Hamm. Smoking and riffling through people's food doesn't mix well either, so Simon Monk had never been a smoker.

I was the only one not smoking on the patio, a bit of a slip. We all slip though; slipping isn't the problem. Trying too hard to correct the slip, that's where you're made.

I was drinking my third Scotch and Soda. Three was a good place to be at, enough that I could seem relaxed but not enough that I start pronouncing aluminum aluminium or anything else. The trick now would be to hold myself at this level of buzz for the rest of the night. Two virgin colas in the next forty-five minutes, one trip to the bathroom, then another Scotch. Rinse and repeat.

There was a large man named Craig Pollard on the other side of the patio auditioning for the role of the party drunk, uncontested, though still fighting the race with all his might. He was tall and heavy and battled to keep himself clean-shaven from the neck up to look as professional as possible throughout the day, but had an inordinate amount of multicolored body hair, with patches of fiery red and deep brown with a streak of white down his back. I knew this from my second night in San Diego, when he'd insisted on showing me the town and we'd ended up at three different full-nude bars. Each of these bars he'd snuck vodka into and insisted that I joined him in his libations. At the third one he'd insisted on buying me a lap dance, wherein a young girl with a badly concealed caesarean scar stared at me with dull uninterested eyes while trying (and failing) to make me erect. It was my first hint that life in San Diego was going to be frustrating, a portent proven true many times since.

Not long after that Craig had attempted to bring me to ComiCon, but that was where I had drawn the line. I give up a lot for this job, but I have not and will not go that deep into cover. If you stare into the abyss, and all that jive.

At the moment, Craig was surrounded by four interns who were marvelling both at his ability to hold his liquor and the fact that his beard seemed to have started to grow in in the brief time since the party had started. He had half a four-ounce steak in his left hand and would take a large bite absently when he felt like it, eating it as though it were a party favor.

One of the interns was a young woman named Cecilia, whom Craig had been covertly trying to get into bed for some time. Covertly for Craig, I mean, by which I mean that he hadn't openly approached her and asked her for intercourse.

I found myself staring at him. He was crass, and spoke using long words that he used properly but pronounced poorly. The three young men that looked at him did so with awe and respect as they asked him about his department's quarterly income figures. Cecilia was staring at him with doe eyes that seemed to take up her entire face. She was wearing a purple dress that sparkled and a perfume that danced on the night air. Craig turned and smiled at me and raised his glass; I smiled and nodded curtly back at him.

"I bet you could steal her away, if you went over," a woman said, siding up alongside me. There was a menthol cigarette clasped between her lips like a leg in a bear trap, the filter nearly crushed between those pursed red lines. Her hair was up 'and held together with pins and a net. She wore a blazer with the collar undone, and a skirt, and looked smart. She wore a broach the same color as her lips. Crimson.

I turned my head to face her. It was Lydia Carter,

Tyler's wife. She was in the prime age to be a successful woman: too old to be a trophy wife, but not so old that she'd lose her husband to one. Not that Tyler has struck me as that sort anyway. They'd married at nineteen, when he was just an investment banker, or so he was fond of telling you when the subject of relationships came up.

She had been watching me for the better part of an hour. I caught her eye when I went back for my second Scotch and Soda, as I'd walked right past the group she was huddled into. A pack of lions, protecting their lionesses. As I said, everyone at the party had been dressed casually: pascal blues and pinks for the men, evening social wear for the women. In my black-and-whites I must have stood out like a sore thumb, or more appropriately, like a zebra. She'd pointed to me and asked Tyler who I was; he'd answered something I couldn't hear. I couldn't hear any of it actually, but body language is quite telegraphic at times.

She'd tried to approach me to say hello while I was on my way back from getting my third (and current) drink, but I'd managed to avoid her by placing a server between us. She'd stood there with her hand outstretched and light dancing in her eyes for a moment, like something motion-captured, and I'd known it was time to make my way out to the balcony and get some fresh, nicotine-saturated air.

Hence the slip, but not a slip.

And now here we were, the wind from the updraft catching a few stray wisps of her hair, and my tie. I turned away from Craig and looked at her, my drink caught half-way between my belly and my mouth. My mouth gaped a little at her beauty, quite deliberately. I turned from her to

Craig and Cecilia the Intern again for a moment, as if not completely sure what she was talking about.

"Oh," I chuckled, taking another sip of my drink. "No, I wasn't looking at her."

Her eyes darted across me, up and down, finding their way to the empty ring finger that helped hold my glass. There were no tan lines from where one had been edged off, no green marks from cheap gold. Her eyes wandered a little beyond that, but not much, and even now I don't know if it had been an act to hide that she was looking for a wedding band or not. "She seems like a perfectly nice young woman," she said finally, turning away from me and sharing in my gaze across at them.

I paused. I'd known the words I'd use before she'd even walked over, before the party had even begun. Now all there was was the timing of them. "Young is the operative word."

She raised an eyebrow at me. I pretended not to notice.

"I'm not looking to get that kind of reputation around the office anyway," I continued with feigned levity, chuckling. "And I'm certainly not ready to settle down."

Her eyes locked onto mine and waited for me to turn. I took another swallow of my drink, counted to ten, and then did. All perfectly planned and rehearsed. Like a scene from a play.

All the best disasters start out that way.

"My name is Lydia Tyler," she said, extending a hand to me the way women in movies about the forties did. I took it and shook it once, firmly, the way I would have shaken a man's hand. I respected her, I respected what she did and how she did it – not that she knew that yet. Her hand was like spun silk or velvet, smooth with flighty fingers that even then tickled the inside of my wrist.

"Simon Monk," I said, smiling at her graciously. I took another sip from my drink and then placed it precariously on the banister of the balcony, so that there was nothing between us but the night. "Pleasure."

She beamed honestly, her cheeks red and healthy. She still kept eye contact with me, as though I were the only thing in the room. Not a lioness, it seemed, but a cougar. "The pleasure is all mine," she said, folding her hands before her.

I was eighteen months deep cover at Shane Industries when I finally got my first real in. Eighteen months.

CHAPTER TWO

There was a thick glass wall close to the main floor bar that was covered in evenly spaced rectangular notches. Each notch held a spoon with a taste of a different dessert on it, the epitaph of the trend towards smaller portions in fine dining. At least it was free. Behind it was a ledge that ran all the way along the windowed wall and was cool and refreshing and looked out onto the sparkling city below.

It was possibly the most romantic spot on the west coast.

My shirt had become undone at some point, the knot of my tie loose and clinging to life near my nipple. My sixth Scotch and Soda was in my hand, and I was using it to mark time.

Lydia was still poised and perfect. She had champagne in her hand that the waiter refilled whenever it was low, moving in and out like a shadow. Even I wouldn't have been able to tell you what he looked like.

We'd been laughing for what seemed like forever and an instant at the same time. Lydia laughed truly and hon-estly, her chest heaving and her mouth taking up most of her face. She laughed the way children laugh, teenagers caught up in a whirlwind of flirtation they don't yet know is flirtation, playing games without subtext and without manipulation. Patty-Cake behind the pitcher's mound.

One story had parlayed seamlessly into the next so that there was no chance to catch our breath or realize how much time was passing.

Her champagne glass dangled precariously near her lips as her laughter faded again, and she looked at me side-on with those soulful eyes from beneath those perfectly preened lashes. "You must have been such a cad," she said slyly before taking another sip. "I'll bet the waitresses were all over you."

I laughed and tweaked my nose with my thumb and tuned away. It was a practised move, one of thirty fake-tells that had been repeated and endorsed until they became second nature. Nothing is as it seems, nothing fits where it's supposed to go. I stared out the window at the blinking red light of a control tower off in the distance and counted to ten. She must have thought I was looking at the stars and didn't move to follow my gaze. Her eyes have been locked intently – hungrily – on mine every since she approached me on the balcony.

I smirked. She leaned her head in every so slightly, tilting it to one side. I turned, made eye contact, and let the smirk grow into a smile. "Okay, there was one."

"Ha ha, I knew it!" she bellowed, uncaring of anyone who might hear. She slapped my knee playfully – an electric feeling that shattered the touch barrier. Outside the moon was big and full and bright orange, a hunter's moon. Focus. "Cad."

"Now," I objected, holding up one finger of the hand

that was cradling the scotch by the brim. "It wasn't like that."

"Sure it wasn't."

I snorted. It's a hard thing to fake and takes a lot of practice. The act is like self-inflicted water boarding. "It wasn't. Honestly. And it wasn't a waitress, it was a hostess."

"What's a hostess?"

"The girl that greets you at the door and take you to your table."

"That's not a waitress?"

"Not if she doesn't take orders," I mumbled and finished my drink. A waiter eyed me and I waved him off with two fingers, quickly and discreetly.

She hummed. She was getting buzzed. She was also getting brave, leaning against the ledge now and casting her eye out over the crowd. She was looking for someone, but didn't find whoever it was. Her husband more than likely. Was she looking to make sure he wasn't watching, or was she looking *hoping* that he was watching? I did not know. All people, and all women especially, desire attention. The only mitigating factor was the type of attention they enjoyed most, consciously or unconsciously. Was Lydia Carter seeking the attention of a new lover or the attention of a jealous husband? In any event, the result is the same and the answer requires a deeper knowledge of psychology and sexual dynamics than I wish to have or employ.

"So this... Hostess," she said the word begrudgingly, as though it were distasteful to her. "Let me guess: tall, blonde, legs that go all the way up to Canada?"

"Now..."

"Sordid affairs in back rooms and dark freezers with strawberries and cream and cheesecake?"

I laughed, this time for real. I clipped it off though; real laughter can be a problem. Real laughter, once heard enough times, can make it far, far too obvious when fake laughter is being employed.

"Her name was Chanelle," I began, swallowing.

"Chanelle? Oh, I like her already. I see a good home-spun girl whose Daddy warned her about men like you."

A controlled laugh. "She was blonde, she wasn't tall though. That was actually how we met."

"You met because she was short?" Lydia finished her champagne and immediately motioned for another. The waiter produced it immediately, as if from air, and provided me with another Scotch and Soda as well, although one had not been requested. I'd have to nurse it now, but try not to make it obvious that I was nursing it.

"There was a jug on a high shelf she was trying to reach. She was jumping for it and trying to knock it down." I paused, taking a moment to try and be as delicate as possible. "She had... copious secondary sexual characteristics," I said, cupping my hands before me to mime what I meant.

Lydia laughed.

"So the kitchen staff wasn't helping her, they were just watching her jump for this jug. When I saw this, I, being a gentleman, retrieved the jug for her."

"And that was when she confessed to you about being good home-spun girl whose Daddy warned her about men like you and you started a sordid affair in back rooms and dark freezers with strawberries and cream and cheesecake."

"No, we rarely spoke until my last night at the restaurant."

"Ooooh, the last night. Those are always good stories. 'Come here, sir, I need to give you something to remember me by.' Ha."

She was being purposefully crass now, and was enjoying herself. Without even trying I realized that she'd been that girl, some years ago now, having affairs in closets and empty bathroom stalls. There was an age limit of such behavior to get the result that women wanted, to make a man feel as though this was his luckiest night on earth. You couldn't enjoy that level of attention as an attractive older woman, no matter how hard you tried to play the game. You could get a man lucky, but you could never be a man's lotto-win again. And there was a fierceness in a man when he'd just won the lotto, a manic energy that surges and is spontaneous and deadly and contagious. It's in his eyes and his hands and his heart, blood pumping, sweat dripping, everything exactly as it should.

Her eyes danced over the crowd for her husband again, and it suddenly struck me how unfair it all was. If a man wanted to "win the lottery" again, he could just play another ticket, to continue the metaphor. But Lydia had *been* the ticket, and now could not be anymore, and was thus shut out of the experience. What a horribly cruel twist of fate that the ones who are best at the game – in fact, the ones for whom the game even exists at all – are the first ones disqualified.

"There was this tradition in the back of house. I knew

about it, but I never thought they'd do it to me. Anyone leaving, they nab and drag out into the alley out back and they pour freezing water over them, and then they pour flour over them."

Lydia's hands went to her mouth and she started laughing again. There was lipstick on her palms now. "Oh my god!"

"Ruined a perfectly good suit."

"Oh my god!!"

"So then, later in the night, Chanelle comes by to say goodbye to me when I'm in the freezer... and one thing did lead to another."

"Ha. I told you. Freezer," she chimed triumphantly.

I nodded. "Yes, well, nothing happened. Nothing to write home about anyway. But she didn't realize until she got home that night that she spent the rest of her shift with my handprints on the back of her pants in flour." I laughed at that. Lydia did too.

There actually had been a Chanelle. She'd been cute and sweet and had always had highlights in her hair at obvious and unprofessional places. She'd been exceptionally uncomfortable about those secondary sexual characteristics I mentioned, and often walked with a tray in front of her even though she never once took an order or delivered a drink. Camouflage was the art of making something that didn't belong look as though it did.

"Oh that poor girl," Lydia said, her laughter trailing off as she wiped her eyes. "Was she young?"

Truth comes quickly and without thought, but can get you in trouble. Tailored responses and selective honesty is better, but requires a level of insight I don't always possess. What was she looking for me to be here? Did she want me to be the caddish cradle-robber that could have any woman he wanted but chose to be with her? Or did she want me to be the mature man, interested chiefly in her type and ilk, for whom chasing a younger woman would be unappealing?

Immediately I realized it's the latter. She wanted to be the lotto ticket again, despite being the skilled hunter. But before I could answer, we were approached.

I almost mistook him for the waiter again, and held up my scotch to let him know I was still drinking the last one he provided me with uninvited.

It wasn't though; it was Tyler Carter.

He lumbered large above me from my position sitting on the floor, his shadow moving past me and falling over the city below. Interesting the way life plays out like metaphors sometimes, isn't it? So many things are only ironic in hindsight.

He regarded me for a moment, then smiled. "Simon."

I nodded and raised my glass to toast him. "Tyler."

Lydia smiled up at him, as though now that he was here, he was the only thing she had eyes for. It was impressive. Switching gears quickly was an art form in and of itself. There were no telltale stutters or stammers as she took Tyler by the arm, squeezed it, and kissed him on the cheek.

I realized with some trepidation that I liked her.

"Simon was just regaling me with stories of managing a restaurant in Idaho."

"Virginia," I corrected out of habit.

"Virginia," she smiled.

"Nothing too scandalous, I hope," Tyler said.

I got to my feet and brushed nonexistent dust off my knees.

"There was an affair with a young waitress."

She had assumed Chanelle was young.

Tyler grinned in that 'you old dog' sort of way that men did at one another and thought that women didn't notice.

"Your wife is a rare woman," I said, touching her gently on the arm. "You're a very lucky man, Tyler." I nodded to her and stepped away without another word, as though Lydia and I had not been deep in conversation, but merely passing ships in the night. Cecilia was by herself at the bar, the lummox she'd been swooning for likely passed out on the bathroom floor by now, and I slid along beside her and ordered a coke. Just a coke this time, nothing else. I left what remained of my alcohol on the bar for the waiter to dispose of.

I kept Lydia and her husband in the corner of my eye. They left soon after, and she threw me a glance over her bare, milky-white shoulder as she did. Her eyes were alive and forgiving and yearning and hungry, even hungrier than they had been when she'd approached me on the balcony.

"Nice tie," Cecilia said, smiling at me with wanton drunken delight. Her eyes were lazy and sleepy.

"It was," I replied. I drained my coke, then made for the exit.

CHAPTER THREE

People think they know what deep cover is and they don't. They think they know because they watched that one Val Kilmer movie where he goes home at the end of the day and tries on different mustaches and suddenly he's speaking in a Russian accent. People think deep cover is just another part of your suit you take off at the end of your workday.

With deep cover, the suit is never off. You go home and you are deep cover. You take a shower and you are deep cover. You take a shit, you are deep cover. You stay deep cover because if you stop once – even for a second – it's too easy to slip back into what you were before. Too easy to curse in your mother tongue if you stub your toe, or turn your head when somebody says the wrong name on a crowded subway.

I got home close to 4 AM from the party sober. My younger self hates me – he cannot imagine ever remembering how I got back from a party. But even that memory, that nostalgia, is a construction, because having been a wild child is a part of a wunderkind in the new millennium business world.

Have you ever told a lie so often you forget it is one?

Maybe you told your friends you lost your virginity to Sally Plain-and-Tall when you were seventeen, when really it wasn't until you were twenty-one and wasn't to Sally, it was to Mary? But you've told the story and pictured it in your head for so many years that now you fool yourself. That is deep cover, but instead it's for your favorite food. For the way you speak. For the way you like to fuck.

I got home and I took off my tie and I laid it down against the green chair. It was a one-bedroom apartment with a small bedroom and a large living room with very little furniture in it. I liked being able to see all of it at once, like an infant being swaddled: I knew my boundaries. I showered and brushed my teeth and put clean pajamas in the dryer to heat them for when I put them on. The apartment was often cold at night.

You never practice deep cover. You are just it. There is never one moment, never one instant when you are not. Nobody can see you practicing reciting all your ex-girlfriends in front of a mirror so you can keep them in order. You have to know all of that – all of it – before you go. Hesitation is key, learning the right amount. Too much and it seems like you're making it up, too little and it seems like you're reciting regurgitated lines.

I took out my phone, a last-model Apple. Whatever was trendy at the time. I punched in my password – 0852 – and there was a message from Lydia. There would have been no indication of the message had I not put in the password. She had written: "This is Lydia. I didn't get the chance to thank you, I had a great evening."

I had not given her my number, intentionally. This was a game of chess that was more like a game of dominoes, in

which the moves you made at the start could inflict causa-
tions which you had no way of stopping. You had to be
careful and deliberate. I thought that way then.

It was a gambit not giving her my number. I could not
ask her for hers: far too typical an approach toward a married woman. Power is as much at play as flirtation -- in
asking for her number, I would be asking for something
of her. The power of the next move would be in my hands
then. To ask a powerful woman for her number is to ask
her to submit to your will. But I equally could not offer
her mine: I could not surrender. If she wanted me to be the
hunter, I could not act the prey. I didn't know what she
wanted from me yet; there wasn't enough information.
But doing nothing risked that first real lead in eighteen
months. Eighteen months of going home smelling like
grease and funneling money into failing businesses.

I looked at my watch. It had been two hours since I had
left the party. Two hours in which she had gotten home –
drunk and giddy – and found my number, on Facebook
or on my resume site or on the company directory. I assumed the latter: she was business-minded and her head
would go the business solutions.

"Me too ;)," I texted back, and waited for the anima-
tion to leave.

The result was instantaneous: ":)"

I waited, and said nothing. I made myself French
toast.

The bread was beginning to crisp when she said: "You
never did mention the waitress's age."

"What waitress?"

"Hostess*"

I paused. "She was in her thirties."

Chanelle had been twenty-two. She'd been finishing her GED and had had aspirations of one day being an advertiser, specifically for books. She thought that if *Fifty Shades* could have been marketed to more copies sold than anything else, than anything could be. She'd never actually read *Fifty Shades* though, only the cheap supermarket romance novellas that people said *Fifty Shades* was. She read them while sitting on a chair in the back hall of the restaurant and sometimes – just sometimes – would get so into the story that she would relax and let the book fall comfortably into her lap, exposing her cleavage to the ogling stares of the servers stepping by.

There was a several minutes pause. When she came back with the simple "okay" like I had suspected she would, I was almost done my toast. I ate it dry, without syrup. When I was completely done, I took two orange gel capsules I kept in the pantry by the fridge and swallowed them with a small glass of ice water.

I knew the conversation was over. I pressed the button on the top of my phone and turned it off, then pressed it on again and typed in my password – 2580. There were different apps now, none of them the same. There was no Candy Crush or Fruit Ninja or Bloons. I opened up the text app and punched in a number; there were no contacts. Remembering telephone numbers is a skill lost to the digital age one has to resurrect when one is deep cover.

I typed, "Contact," then shut off the phone and went to bed, and dreamed the dreams of a man I never was and would never really, truly be. That is what it means to be deep cover.

I had not dreamed my own dreams for eighteen months.

CHAPTER FOUR

The next move happened fast. It had to. While emotions can linger for years or even decades, if one wants action and movement, you have to strike while the iron's hot.

Six days later, I was at the weekly staff meeting. Weekly staff meetings at major companies are exercises in masturbation: pictures and graphs and charts to illustrate how good each of us were at doing what we were paid to do that week. It is the grown-up equivalent of presenting your hastily drawn macaroni art to your mother for display on the door of the fridge.

I paid little attention to the numbers or the charts or the trends. Great leaps in success of companies that have already topped the one billion mark in pre-tax revenue rarely came from such minor factors. Once you grew so large that you were a part of the culture, it took great epistemic shifts within that culture to truly affect you.

I paid great attention, however, to the presenters. How much trouble did the peacocks go through to display their feathers in front of their master? Tyler sat at the back of the room and watched, making a note on the pad in front of him every once and a while. Were he and I the only ones really watching, actively listening? Were we watching for the same things, I wondered at the time. I suspected then that we were not, that he was hunting for some forbidden pattern in the numbers in front of him. I suspect now, perhaps, that he was looking the same as me.

The people that presented wore their hearts on their sleeves. I took notes on the numbers and discarded the paper immediately afterward. I took mental notes and filed them away forever. David was exhausted and fumbled his way through his presentation, but not because of alcohol or drugs. His eyes were never red, even deep in the corners where the Visine didn't help. He didn't stumble on every word, but always the same words: long syllables, usually with a 'b'. I decided at once it was a combination of nerves and the re-emergence of a long-dormant stammer. It would pass on its own. David worked for Shane, and you didn't get there by being weak or lacking confidence; therefore, his nerves were not caused by his work. Stress in the home life then – not kids; work provided an escape from kids. I narrowed in on issues with the wife or the soon-expected death of a parent. It went in the file without judgement. The file isn't for judgements; it's for information.

Craig had been drunk, but not recently. It was still in his pores. He was the one I'd been waiting for, the real act to follow. I wanted to impress – to leave an impression – and to do it, I needed to follow a weak performance. This was chess played with thin paper pieces, where even gripping them too hard would make them crumble and become useless. Seduction, no matter the method, is a delicate art.

I waited for Craig to finish talking about the boost his work caused in pre-tax revenue in the hardware division, a difference of cents on the millions, and said:

"Moon landing."

Eyes turned to me, as though I'd been invisible the entire time. I had been.

"Simon, something to say?" Tyler asked, punctuating his syllables with his pen.

I pretended to look surprised. I held my breath for a moment – heart rate increased, cheeks slightly flushed. "Oh, sorry. I've been doing research into this new company out of Virginia. Hometown boys, you know how it is. They've been working on this new hardware, much smaller than the stuff on the market today, but faster. They've been working on it in their basement and living off Kickstarters. They call it Moon Landing."

It was the most I'd spoken all at once in weeks. It was almost exhausting. Exposition always is.

"The things they're trying... well, it'd be great, if it worked. That's a big if though. The money you're saving, Craig," I turn to Craig. "I was just thinking we could invest there. Cents on the dollar don't mean much to us, but to start-ups... well, we remember."

None of them remembered.

"Anyway, sorry. Not the place. Sorry to interrupt."

Craig finished his presentation as Tyler scribbled a note onto the pad in front of him. As soon as I'm out of the meeting, I turned on my phone and texted, "Moon Landing."

It was time to trigger an epistemic shift.

CHAPTER FIVE

See, all it takes is money, and knowing where the holes in the system are. That and people: you need a lot of people to act in just the right way for just the right amount of time.

Since the dawn of the Internet age, the stock exchange has changed so dramatically that nobody except the extremely wealthy can really trade stocks fairly anymore. It's an industry that relies heavily on speed: how fast can I act? Back in the day when all the traders were on one floor, that amounted to who could talk the fastest and the loudest to be heard. Now though, that speed isn't measured in minutes, but seconds. Not seconds, but microseconds. Not microseconds, but *nano*seconds. These distances are imperceptible to the human eye, but to a computer they matter immensely. Stock brokers pay big money to have their computer just a few feet closer to the server, trying to shave off as many tenths of a nano as they can. Private fibre-op lines are built to be as straight as they could so that packets of information aren't diverted.

All this is simple enough. It's hard to understand in such small terms, but if you squint your eyes and tilt your head sideways, you can kind of see what happened. But a few years ago, somebody really figured out how to exploit the system.

See when you buy a lot of stock on your computer, that order is broken up and sent to different exchanges all around the country – so it arrives at those exchanges at slightly different times. We're talking about thousandths of a second in the difference. Some of them go to New York and some of them go to Florida. Here's the trick: when New York gets a big order, it sends a message to Florida to let it know, and that message goes over their own high-speed connection. The warning arrives before your order does, and Florida knows to jack up the price of that stock. Now your money doesn't buy you as much. All that in the time it took you to click your mouse.

Essentially what this did was make it very hard for normal people – people who were not high-frequency traders – to make any money in the stock market. The system was usurped to work against you. What it did do, however, is make it extremely easy to *lose* a lot of money in the stock market.

Every time New York receives a large volume of purchases on a specific stock, and recognizes that action as just its portion of a much larger order, it sends that information off to Florida and they jack up the price. Click the buy button, then click the refresh button: uh-oh, you just paid more for your stock than you had intended to. Now the stock costs more, up to $1.08 a share from $1.06. Click 'buy' again, the same thing. It recognizes the trend, now it's at $1.13, a bigger jump than the last time. Each of these clicks represents huge transactions, thousands of dollars each. Tens of thousands more than likely.

I never ask how much money it takes. I don't want to know. I know it's enough that I can really only pull this trick once.

I watched the stock slowly rise, inch by inch, dollar by dollar. The transactions followed the Fibonacci numbers: the second purchase two minutes after the first, the second three minutes after that, the third five minutes after that, and so on. Two hours into our little pattern, there was a purchase out of order, a large one. The stock jumped. The new buyer, the one that wasn't a part of the pattern, went through at 3pm.

I dearly hoped it was Tyler, because immediately afterward the purchases came in rapid succession – as fast as they could be processed. At the time of the out-of-order purchase, the stock was at $5.08 a share. By the time the frenzy of buying was complete and the market closed, it was well over $10.

Eighteen months of unbelievably pedantic meetings and so many tens of thousands of dollars I didn't even want to think about it, all to potentially double the worth of Tyler Carter's personal stock portfolio. Tens of thousands of dollars just to impress a little man with a big hat enough that he'd mention me in passing to his wife.

CHAPTER SIX

The following Friday I was at a bar in downtown San Diego called Theories. It was dark and the carpet was poorly kept, and there were framed theoretical phrases every few feet along the wall with misaligned faded stock-photos of molecules in the backgrounds of each. These phrases ranged from the intellectual to the absurd:

Velocity equals the Hubble constant times distance.

$E = mc2$

If I fill my mouth with soda and ice cream, my brain will stop from brain freeze even if the soda was warm.

Things like that. There was a long bar and a dance floor that nobody danced at even though the music was impossibly loud, and roughly thirty pool tables. There were blue lights, but not nearly enough of them on, and children drinking far too much alcohol in the corner. One of them might have been old enough to get a learner's permit, and two were still clutching the book bags they'd brought to school with them, yet the bartender still hadn't carded them. They eyed everyone else in the bar suspiciously through secretive glances, as though constantly afraid that they would soon be caught and asked to leave.

I'd gone to Theories with Craig after work. Actually,

that's a bit of an oversimplification: we had gone from work to Stompers, a restaurant that seemed to think it could get around various health-code violations by marketing itself instead as an 'eatery.' We had gone from Stompers to Liquid, Liquid to Flappers, Flappers to Wild Ones, and Wild Ones to Theories.

Liquid had been posh and upscale, and had it been twenty years earlier, I would have said that everyone there had been on cocaine. As it was, I wasn't quite sure what breed of drug they were on.

Flappers had been a VIP bar that we'd gotten into by virtue of our position and dress, but had received so many dirty looks thanks to Craig's boisterous humor that we'd been asked to leave after only three over-priced drinks. Cecilia had met us outside of Flappers and had followed us to Wild Ones and Theories. I could only assume that Craig had messaged her to tell her to come join us, though for the life of me I had no idea when. As far as I could tell, he hadn't even taken out his phone all night.

Wild Ones was an unnamed Irish bar next to a strip club, the name clearly applying to the strip club alone. Cecilia refused to go into the strip club half and I played the part of the gentleman by stubbornly agreeing with her, although there was nothing gentlemanly about it in truth. I was gravely concerned that Craig would try to order me a lap dance and that I would have to try and talk my way out of it. And so, outvoted, the three of us stayed on the Irish side of the bar with Craig craning his head to see the topless wonders that lay just beyond his reach until, finally, he gave up and suggested that we head to Theories.

I was having considerable difficulty maintaining the

proper level of buzz through all of this, in large part due to Craig's destructive machinations. I had had my three Scotch and Sodas – that hadn't been an issue. I had even managed to have one virgin cola afterward, even though Craig tried to accompany me each and every time I went to the bar to order. But when my first virgin drink was running low, Craig took it upon himself to order tequila shots, followed by something with a name that sounded like a pornographic movie title, followed by the return of my Scotch and Soda, one for each of the three of us.

It quickly became impossible to control and moderate the level of drunk I was becoming, and I resolved to switch to virgin whenever I could sneak one past Craig – the issue was if he was not absent enough, I would get too drunk, and if he was absent too much, I would get too sober. The latter might not seem like an issue, but it could prove a dead giveaway if the situation turned. Despite what some actors will tell you, there is no perfect way to falsify an alcoholic stupor.

But there was very little hope of that happening; Craig rarely left my side and when he did it was to urinate, leaving Cecilia with me, always with instructions to "keep my hands off" followed by hearty claps on the back and strained chuckles from me. My vision was becoming unbalanced, and I resolved to try and avoid words that I might, in my inebriated state, pronounce incorrectly. Whenever possible, say 'home' instead of 'house,' 'leave' instead of 'out,' and under no circumstances talk about a certain malleable metal sheet that one can use to cover food or protect one's thoughts from alien invaders.

You might be wondering why I agreed to this if it's

truly as much work as I'm making it out to be. And while it was true that barhopping with Craig was a lot like trying to care for a three hundred pound hungry toddler with Asperger's, it was something that a reasonable person would see as 'fun'. And 'fun' was a part of the personality that I desperately needed to protect and cling to, especially at this delicate stage of my plans.

You see, it wasn't just enough for me to be good at my job. Loads of people are good at their jobs, but very few of them are also likable. Many of them spend their days running TPS reports twelve hours a day, only get paid for eight, and then retire to the colourful world of an MMRPG for a few hours before knocking out for bed and starting the whole process all over again, only breaking the schedule when alcohol and desperate loneliness somehow produced overweight children. I couldn't be that: I had to be good at the job, and also be liked by those at the job, which translated into having to be *very* good at the job so that I would have enough time left over after having done the job in order to form the social connections needed to be liked at the job. Most Type-A personalities trying to accomplish this do so out of some self-gratifying need to be liked or need to be needed, and even then not without copious amounts of uppers.

I had to do this while remaining relatively drug-free, *and* doing the actual job of remaining in deep cover.

And the truth was I did like Craig – he was awkward in a way that he somehow owned. Was he obnoxious? Yes. Loud? Yes. Insistent? Naturally. But somehow still very likable. I think I envied him on some level, the way he careened from one moment to the next without so much as a thought or a plan; so different from the way I was forced to live. Craig was honest in a way I could never be and off-putting in a way I had never been. I'm not sure that I ever enjoyed being in his company, but it was certainly easier to feign enjoyment around him.

It was also easier to hide in his shadow. Craig was loud, and always over-spoke and under-thought, making it easy for anyone around him to simply blend in. In some strange way he became a part of my deep cover, one of the tools within my toolbox, like a jackhammer – yes, rarely used, but effective when it needed to be.

"Yeah!" he yelled, clapping his hands loudly at the end of 'Cotton-Eyed Joe,' as though the members of Rednex could hear his appreciation for them from wherever they were. When he lowered his hands, one of them clapped me on the back, and he arose. "I need to take a piss."

I nodded and held up my glass to him; he nodded back and stumbled towards the loo.

Cecilia stared at me from across the table. This had happened several times throughout the night, those awkward moments when two people who would have otherwise not associated were forced to make conversation with one another. I suppose we could have just ignored one another, but that could have proven problematic. The corners of her mouth twitched, her pupils floating in a gutter of alcohol that had permeated her body. "I slept with him," she said finally, matter-of-factly.

I raised my eyebrows and nodded.

This was actually the third time she had made the same admission to me, which gave a strong indication of just how drunk Cecilia really was. The first time had been after he had jumped the eight when playing pool to sink the six when caught in a tight corner, and had been said with pride and admiration. The second time had been after I had done something (I'm not sure what) that had presumably caused her to think that I was looking at a woman on the other side of the bar. That time it had been said as a gloat, in an "I'm getting something you're not" sort of fashion. This time it was with a twinge of regret, as though she was saying it to a priest during a confession. The depressant we were all drinking must have been getting to her, I decided.

"I haven't told my boyfriend," she said.

This information was new, but not unexpected. The way Cecilia had looked at Craig at the Christmas party, it had not been in the way one looked at someone when they saw something they want. It was the way they looked at someone when they saw something they wanted that they weren't currently getting. A subtle difference, but an important one. Still, she was young, and there would be plenty of mistakes ahead. We've made more than a few.

"I don't think I'm going to," she said, her brow furrowing into a tiny wrinkle between her eyebrows. It vanished as she relaxed, and I saw that that would be a permanent fixture of her face as she aged. A wrinkle, perhaps even her first wrinkle.

"That's up to you," I nodded at her, listing my glass to my lips and then placing it back down again. It occurred to me suddenly that I might be able to find some excuse to dispose of the remainder of my drink now, while Craig was in the bathroom. Was Cecilia drinking the same thing I was? And if so, was she too drunk to notice if I poured the remainder of my beverage into her glass? When I looked, I saw that Cecilia's previously cola-saturated drink had been replaced with a deep blue one that could have only been an Aqua-Velva, and curled my lip in disgust before taking another sip of my drink.

"Have you ever cheated?"

She asked me this devoid of context, her voice trailing upward at the end of the word 'cheated' and making the query sound like something hopeful. Hopeful for what, I wondered. My brain was moving too sluggishly; it was discouraging. I had to stop this rapid consumption of alcohol in different types and quantities, and wondered all at once if I had it in me to feign some sort of alcohol poisoning event. Did she want me to be the saint who would never do such a thing, the scoundrel who had done it often and enjoyed it, or the mourner who did it once and always lived to regret it? Did it matter?

The fact that I asked myself the latter truly signifies how intoxicated I was becoming. Everything matters when you're in deep cover, you never know what might come back to bite you in the ass. You are always on, and every answer matters. I decided I would need to get out of there soon.

"No," I said finally, and did not elaborate. Was it true? It's difficult to say, so difficult that even I would have a hard time telling you with great certainty and great honesty. When one lies for a living, there become problems with matters of discerning the truth, and as this was not a steadfast fact like 'Where were you born,' there was some interpretation involved.

Craig returned then, with three deep brown drinks in

small squat glasses and laid one of them in front of each of us. He clapped me on the back again; this was how I marked his comings and goings. His hand had still been wet, and I could feel the moisture from it against my suit. "Finish that quick, so we can all get started on these at once," he said, motioning to my Scotch and Cecilia's Aqua-Velva.

Cecilia downed hers in one gulp, and I reluctantly followed suit.

We played a game of billiards that I found incredibly hard to follow. There were three of us, so I swear we started by playing nine-ball, but at some point during the game, I remember looking down and realizing that the bright yellow sphere that was the nine-ball was no longer on the table, and yet we were continuing to play. There were also tens and elevens, so I deduced that we were actually playing eight ball.

What followed was a thirty-minute period during which I tried to discern exactly which brand of eight ball we were playing. At one point I had to shoot a scratch from behind the line, while at another I was afforded a ball-in-hand. At some point I resolved to simply bounce the balls around the table at varying speeds until Craig clapped me on the back and informed me that I'd lost. This, in turn, was followed by another round of shots named after a minor celebrity and another round of drinks supplied by Craig – Aqua-Velva's all around, this time.

My body's ability to abide alcohol can only go so far. As such, as you might have guessed, there are large portions of that evening which I do not currently have access to. I can only assume that at some point, later down the road, those memories will dislodge like a leaf caught on a rock in a stream and I will become privy to the fact that, yes – I did spend the better part of five-minutes discussing politics with Cecilia's chest, or some other such dubious action I would have otherwise abhorred.

We were sitting around a small round table, the seats of which were impossibly high and impossibly small and hard to balance on, when I came to the sudden realization that I had to get out of there.

Everything was blurring around me, all of the lights created lens flares on my retinas. Craig was talking about one of the theories on the wall – a hipster joke involving dating, which may or may not have been attributed to "The Bro Code." Cecilia was laughing honestly. There were people around – far, far more people than there had been when we'd entered. Was it still the same night? Was this bar ever going to bloody close?

Billiards. Loo. Bloody- fuck, I wasn't thinking in the right tongue, I realized, and forced myself to stand up from the table in the middle of Craig's sentence.

He looked at me, his eyes soft and concerned. "You okay, buddy?"

I must have made more of a scene than I'd intended to. "I'm fine," I said as I nodded, or perhaps I just nodded. "I just need to hit the... the... need to pee." I couldn't say bathroom. I was trying to, but all that wanted to come out was loo. How had I allowed myself to get so bloody fucked?

"Do you need me to come with you?" he asked, still concerned.

Oh God, I realized. *We're friends.* I shook my head, he

nodded, and I turned and made my way to the wash-room.

There was a theory framed above each of the urinals. Mine read that if there was a small defect or crack etched into the bowl of a urinal, men would attempt to aim for it and therefore spill less. I looked down and – sure enough – there was an image of a fly tattooed into the bowl I was currently urinating into, and the hot liquid that streamed out of me was cascading all around it. I wondered – likely for too long – if telling a man about that particular theory lessened its affect, like telling someone that you were prescribing them a placebo for their back pain: if you tell them, you've defeated the purpose.

I leaned my head against the clear plastic of the theory and waited until I was done. It seemed to take far longer than it should have. When I was finally done making water, I carefully tucked myself back into my trousers, washed my hands, and took out my phone. With great effort – and multiple attempts – I punched in 0852. There was a message from Lydia. I decided now would not be the best time to answer it, shook myself sober as much as I could, and headed back out into the bar proper.

I spied Craig and Cecilia across the room and realized I could just leave. I certainly had my facilities about me enough that I could sneak past the likes of Craig Pollard. I could leave, get back out into the night air, and find a cab to take me home. Certainly not the friendliest thing to do under the circumstances, but being slightly inconsiderate was a minor offense when one was blatantly, blisteringly drunk.

"Are you okay?" said the woman in front of me. I

turned and made eye contact with her quickly, as my brain took a moment to play catch-up. I'd been staring at Craig and Cecilia, trying to make a choice as to whether to stay or go. This woman had been on her way past me, stopped and backed up into my peripheral vision, and asked if I was okay. She then stepped fully in front of me and asked if I was okay, which I clearly was not.

However, I said: "Yes, sorry, I'm fine."

"Are you sure?" she asked, brushing back dirty-blonde hair. "You don't look well. You're very pale."

I touched my forehead as though I would have been able to feel my paleness, and instead was treated to just how sweat-laden my brow had become. There was a seat not far behind me, and I found myself sitting. This woman's hand was on my arm. She had been guiding me into the chair and I had not even noticed.

"Sit for a moment," she said, and started to fumble with something in her purse. She took out her cell phone, let it bathe her face in pale light for a moment as she typed something, then put it away and returned her gaze to me.

My vision lolled past her head and I saw Craig, lumbering towards me with a drink in each hand. They were red and had fruit sticking out of them and there was some clear disconcerting liquid at the top that refused to mix with the rest. My stomach was already starting to protest this concoction, which I do not know the name of but have dubbed the "Kirstie Alley." It seems fitting, although I am not sure why.

Craig looked up from the drinks and saw me, sitting at the table with this blonde woman. His smile vanished, then reappeared in a different fashion. He backed up several paces without a word, nodding to himself, and sat back down with Cecilia and both drinks.

I looked at the woman with new light: she was a shield. A mystical, magical shield that repelled alcoholic beverages and lumbering idiots. A bartender came over to us and asked if we wanted anything, and she said: "Two virgin colas please."

Oh blessed Madonna! I was saved!

The woman turned back toward me, her hair tumbling in front of her eyes despite her best efforts. "Do you want me to stay with you a minute?" she asked, that same concern in her voice that Craig had voiced just a few moments ago.

Yes, I responded. "I would like that very much."

CHAPTER SEVEN

She told me her name was Maggie and that she worked in accounting, both of which were true. I say that not because anything she said or will say is a lie, but because there are so many lies and half-truths in my life that I have to distinguish when someone uses their *real* name and their *real* occupation. If that strikes you as sad, it's because it is.

Her favorite movie of all-time was *Ferris Beuler's Day-Off*, and she absolutely subscribed to the theory that Ferris was actually a figment of Cameron's imagination, a personification of his Id doing all the things he could never do, including (but not limited to) dating Sloan Peterson. She'd written a thesis paper on it in university during a film study course, which she'd minored in.

"Film Theory and Accounting?" I asked, smiling over the cuff of my suit. I had a tiny pink umbrella in my hand, and no idea how it had gotten there. Evidently I was still quite drunk.

"Mmm-hmm," she hummed. "I was going to be the first accountant to know the exact building cost of the Death Star."

I laughed again.

Unsurprisingly, the Cameron-Ferris Theory was not one of the theories displayed on the wall of the bar.

She told me she'd always liked acting when she was young, and had been in her high-school drama troupe. She'd tried again when she got to university, but had never been good enough to perform at that level. "At that level all I could do was minor in watching actors, not being one.

"Isn't it weird how jocks make fun of all the drama kids, but idolize all the actors?" she asked. She was drinking Virgin Cokes now too, either so that I wouldn't feel bad or so as to not get too inebriated around the complete stranger. Or both. "I mean, all those actors they fawn over are just the drama geeks they called faggot all grown up, right? It's so stupid."

I agreed that it was quite stupid. She said with word 'faggot' with distaste, her lip curling when the word was in her mouth. I adored her for it, and must have smiled. I told her that I had been in drama when I had been young too, as well as sports: the track team, to be precise.

Which was also true.

Not true of the deep cover, not a part of the carefully constructed identity I'd carved for myself since first putting on an apron and learning how to properly manage an allergy-order in a back-of-house kitchen: the real truth.

I wanted a smoke for the first time in years. I felt my shoulders relax, and then roll back. My posture changed, in a way I wasn't quite familiar with, and I was grinning out of the right side of my mouth as I stared across the table at those bright, seafoam-green eyes.

I paused for a moment, wiped my mouth, and said,

"When I was fifteen, I got the lead in the school play. It–"

"Wait, let me guess," she grinned, holding the thumb and forefinger of each hand to make a screen and placing me in it. She had one eye closed and her tongue protruded as she 'focused.' "Thick cheeks, slender jaw, thin eyebrows... Hamlet."

I smiled and shook my head, "No."

"No?"

"No, it was an original play, something one the drama coaches cooked up, thinking they were being the smart auteurs that no high-school drama coach really is." I paused, not wanting to go on if I was boring her. She was watching and listening intently. "It was called *"How Good is It?"* It was about a young boy – moi – who was obsessed with finding out how good sex really was."

Maggie rolled her eyes. "Subtle. Ten bucks says it ends with a teen pregnancy."

I paused, for what must have been a little too long, because her gaze softened as it had when I was stumbling out of the washroom. "... It did," I said finally, smiling. I took another sip of my drink. "Actually, one night while I was rehearsing with the female lead, I confessed to being nervous about a scene where I would have to fake... oh, how shall I put this... Erotic Excitement."

She giggled.

"Of course I was nervous because I'd never had the experience first-hand – which she gratefully provided."

She rolled her eyes at me again, but was smiling. "A cad was born."

I snorted my drink.

It was the most I had spoken in eighteen months without thinking about the game of chess my words were playing. My shoulders relaxed some more, so much so that I felt calcium pop in the nape of my neck. Sometimes, you don't realize how tense life has made you until you finally relax.

We talked about the last election, a usual faux pas among strangers, but it came up organically and neither of us felt the need to artificially swerve the conversation away from it. We held differing political views but neither of us was far enough left or right that we couldn't respect and value what the other had had to say, and I think we both left the experience with more to think about on a few issues. I know I did.

I told her my favorite movie was *The Godfather*, a lie that she called me out on, claiming that "All men say their favorite film is *The Godfather* when their real favorite film would hurt their ego to admit." I admitted that it was a lie and that that was the reason, but would not tell her what the real choice was. She'd have to just take gratification in the fact that she'd done what few others could do, and caught me in a fib.

She told me that she didn't like chocolate, but ate a small piece of dark chocolate every night after dinner, for the antioxidants. She told me she'd had an acne problem as a teen but that it had faded, although she still had some scarring on her cheeks. I told her it wasn't noticeable (this too was a lie, but if she caught me in it she did not mention. What wasn't a lie was that it didn't detract from the overall aesthetic beauty of her face). She told me she listened to something called ASMR on YouTube to relax before bed sometimes, but couldn't remember what the acronym stood for.

Autonomous Sensory Meridian Response, by the way. I looked it up some time later.

I told her that the first time I had been drunk had been at my father's wake, and that I'd spent a great deal of it clutching the toilet off the parapet and vomiting into it while sobbing uncontrollably. This was a partial lie: I had actually been drunk the entire three days from the time of my father's death *until* his wake, on the coin of a good friend. It was not the first drink I had, but it had been the first time I had been drunk. And I hadn't sobbed or cried at all; I'm not sure why I said that.

She told me both her parents were alive, and all of her sisters. She only had one aunt, but they had never been close, and she didn't know now if she was alive or dead. All her grandparents had been dead before she'd been old enough to walk, a consequence of being born late in her parents' lives.

At some point I looked around the bar, and realized it was all-but empty. Craig and Cecilia had left, presumably together. I didn't think they'd come over to announce that they were leaving, but I might have missed it while in the deep troughs of my stupor. The house lights were still down, but the staff was cleaning up for the night.

"Oh," she said, looking around. Apparently she was as surprised as I was. "I guess we should leave."

There was a moment then, when she looked at me and expected me to suggest we leave together.

"I'll get you in a cab," I said, not making a show of it. I wasn't saying it to be gallant, but if it was a gallant thing to say, then all the better. She smiled and nodded.

We stepped outside and found a cab almost immediately, leaving little time for the awkward conversation that would usually accompany such a situation. Would I wait with her, would I just start on my way home? Would I try to split the cab in an effort to segue into sexual congress – all of that bypassed by an efficient cabby. I gave him some money without letting Maggie see how much and told him to make sure she got home. She would have had to live on the moon for it not to have covered tab and tip.

She stood in the door of the cab and looked at me for a long moment. I'm not sure if she was debating asking me to join her, or if she was just trying to find the right words to say goodnight... but I like to think it was the latter. The night had been smooth and easier, easier than any night I'd had in, well, much longer than eighteen months actually. It might have actually been years. I didn't like to think that that experience wasn't a shared one, at least on some level.

I decided to save her the trouble of whatever she was deciding either way. "Thank you for helping me tonight, Maggie."

She smiled and nodded. "I had a great time, Simon," she said, her voice almost lost on the early morning breeze. Then she leaned in and kissed me, ever so fleetingly, on the corner of my mouth. Her thumb had found its way to my cheek and stroked it once before falling away. She ducked into her cab before I could say anything, and was gone.

I stood there as it pulled away, basked in the crisp chill of the winter night. I turned and started my short walk home with a spring in my step and a smile on my face, stopping only once the entire way there to steady myself – as it turned out, despite all her help, I was still quite drunk.

So drunk in fact, that it never occurred to me then that I hadn't told her my name.

CHAPTER EIGHT

The text from Lydia had been precisely what I had hoped it would be.

You see, I couldn't chase her; there was something caddish about that. Going after a married woman includes equal parts of letting her come to you and knowing what to say when she does.

I didn't have that luxury.

Unrealized sexual attraction is something that can hang in the subconscious for years at a time, only to dislodge in the form of an awkward phone call years after the fact after watching a romantic comedy with a few too many poignant scenes. It can take the form of years of cat-and-mouse, with one person's situation becoming desperate enough that they call only to find the other person happy, or vice versa. Years can pass before the two sync up, if they ever do, and the result is almost always disappointing. Very few sexual experiences can live up to ten years of foreplay.

And I'm sure it would have gone that way with Lydia, if I weren't who I am. I might not have heard from her again and been avoided by her at next year's Christmas bash, if she came at all. Tyler would realize the stir within his wife and do something uncharacteristically suave, a vacation more than likely. I would fade into the ether until he inevitably began to ignore her again, and nostalgia would take hold. Would things have been better with that cad, Simon Monk? I might have moved on by then to another job or another position; her desperation might have to reach a fever pitch before she got up the effort to contact me, and even then the dips and rises of marriage might have to make her contact me several times before we actually met. By the time she did, the young lady-killer she'd met at that one Christmas Party would be long dead, replaced by a silver-haired buffoon with too much weight on and sagging jowls.

While my timetable was by no means short, it was nowhere near that long. So a reminder had to be engineered, preferably coming from her husband himself. Necessarily, actually, since social media didn't reveal anyone that might have been better suited to deliver the message for me.

Hence the stock manipulation. By now the stock in the company that owned the rights to Moon Landing had fallen again (the market can't abide the type of inflation I'd facilitated). But the second it started to fall, Tyler Carter would have pulled out. Assuming the initial dip wasn't too severe (and it hadn't been), he would have doubled his already-large sum of money, all based on an off-hand tip that I gave him.

So Tyler Carter, sitting at home much as I was and watching this drama unfold with glee, turns to his wife and says something to the tune of: "That consultant I hired, Simon Monk? I just made a hundred grand off a tip he gave me on the stock market." Or something of the like.

Now that I think about it, it likely went nothing like that. I imagine he was celebrating on his own or calling a friend to tell him to buy while the buying was good as well, when his wife would have taken notice of his excitement and asked what had happened. *Being* excited, he would have had to frame the story from the beginning: he couldn't just tell her he'd made some money; that was boring. He'd have to tell about where it came from, where the idea struck him in that meeting, and whose off-handed comment had sparked it. Yes, my contribution to the story would be minimal from his point of view, but after mentioning my name (and in such a positive, impressive light) the rest of the tale would hold no context for Lydia Carter.

The text itself was more than I'd hoped for, and I suspect that she'd shared in a small bit of her husband's celebratory drink before making it: "Seems like I wasn't the only one impressed with you. ;)"

A text like that from a beautiful older woman would be enough to send any man's mind into a frenzy, especially when said woman happened to be your boss' wife: a prospect with simultaneous feelings of baleful vengeance and fear attached to it. I imagine some young men would analyze the text, possibly with the help of a friend or two, and decide the best course of action going forward. I am not speaking out of experience, unless one counts sitcoms that air on the television screens at the gym as 'experience.'

But in truth, the text still got a fair amount of analyzing from me, though in what I imagine is a far more intellectual fashion. It was hard to find a Lacanian Mirror Stage in a text of only ten words and an emoticon, sure, but I could certainly try.

It was obviously an overwhelmingly positive message, and had I not been in no fit state to do so at the time, I might have responded to it immediately and without much thought. But now that I looked at it, there were troubling elements. Notably, it was in the past tense. She had not written "Seems like I'm not the only one you impressed;" she had written "Seems like I wasn't the only one impressed with you." The difference was subtle but important, even if she wasn't totally aware of what she had said. People very rarely are aware of what they're saying, and it was one of the first traits I had to master when going into deep cover. Tense, tone, and emphasis: all this was vitally important to language.

The past tense was troubling; it indicated that the affair might have been over before it had truly begun. That she *had* been impressed with me, and in the days since moved on to something new or decided that the flirtation had been the drink and nothing else, a harmless bit of fun between strangers.

But if that were totally the case of course, she wouldn't have sent the text at all.

And then there was the wink, the herald of sexual promise of the emoticons. These messages were contradictory and troubling, but overall very positive. Lydia was still on the fence and I'd known that already – had she not been, my deep cover would have been over several days ago and I wouldn't have had the chance to get so drunk with Craig that many of my brain cells had collectively committed suicide rather than bathe in stinging hot alcohol.

I messaged back: "High praise from a rare woman is always appreciated."

Women as beautiful as Lydia have been told they're beautiful from the time they first bled and developed breasts, if not before. As such, the word has lost all meaning. Anyone hoping to actually make a legitimate impression should never use the word beautiful, unless the woman in question was well on her way to sixty and may not have heard it in some years, which Lydia Carter was not. There were several other euphemisms of beautiful, from the all-too-plain 'pretty' to the far-too-extravagant 'radiant,' but a smart man chooses a point of phrase that can hold many meanings for the mind to latch on to.

Beautiful can mean many things; it can even apply to more than aesthetic beauty (though usually not, and almost always in defense of its use). But of the things it can mean, they are solely complimentary and almost all of them are focused on the same attributes a woman has heard commented on since time immortal.

A true compliment, to stay in the mind and dig in its hooks the way one needs it to, should be much more opaque and obtuse than that. It should not be easy to discern its meaning through simple deduction, and perhaps even contain the possibility that it was not meant as a compliment at all. In times past, 'unique woman' might have been an acceptable choice, but unique has been co-opted by the loud, obnoxious manic-pixie dream-girls of the world since its hay-day of high praise and should not be used unless the woman in question embodies those qualities.

I have found 'rare' to be a much better choice. Such a small word, but it contains so much within it, like a small pouch packed to the brim with diamonds. What did it mean? Did it mean that I was beautiful, and in fact so beautiful that I was rare in my beauty? If so, then 'rare' would be better by definition than any of those words describing that beauty could have been. Did it mean that I was intelligent or engaging or witty or funny, and that the rareness of me was that those qualities were found in such a beautiful woman? If so, then 'rare' embodied many complimentary phrases at once and, even better, could embody those that the receiver felt was the most important. If the woman in question had always prided herself on her wit and you complimented her poise, that might fall flat. 'Rare' allowed for individual interpretation and meaning. There was also of course the possibility that it wasn't a compliment at all: was I rare because he's attracted to me despite my not being beautiful? Multiple interpretations, none of which I had any intention of ever expanding upon. Like the monster in a horror movie: the imagination could do more than the reality ever could.

"What are you doing?" she asked, without emotional punctuation.

In truth, I was doing very little: eating unsalted oatmeal and getting ready to swallow two capsules that were far too large for the human throat to withstand without pause. She pictured me watching TV or going over reports or reading a book as I chatted with her, the chat a bit of auxiliary entertainment to the main event of whatever I was doing to unwind after a long day. In truth, I was doing very little *but* scrutinize her texts and the tone of her texts, when compared to those previous. I was, after all, really working for the first time in several days.

"Reading," I lied, a partial lie. I am reading, though not a blog or a book or magazine or a report: I'm reading her texts, her social media posts, my notes on Tyler's behavior, and trying to construct a timeline of her mood and position.

"Reading what? :)"

The smile was a good upgrade. "Hemingway," I answer, upgrading what was first a misleading comment into the realm of total fabrication. I could have spouted any of Hemingway's titles, but nothing would hold the power of the synecdoche of invoking the author's name to stand in for his work as a whole. And of the authors I could have chosen – Hemingway, King, and Grant were all authors my deep cover was intimately familiar with – Earnest would hold the most meaning for a woman as... *rare* as Lydia.

I waited several beats, before adding: "And you?"

"Heading to bed." No emoticon attached. Dangerous invitation. A salacious invitation, or a polite way of ending the conversation?

After several tense moments, I texted back: ";)?"

As strange as it might sound, this was possibly the most daring move I had taken so far. More than my compliments, the disgusting amount of money I had unceremoniously flushed down the toilet to manipulate the stock exchange, or stepping away from Lydia at the party so that she would come out to the balcony to see me; this one, simple text was a very daring move.

I was not only expressing an emotion myself, I was asking her to impress one. Nay, I was actually placing the words into her mouth, and asking if I was correct in doing so. She had initially let the context of the comment hang, but I was forcing her to assign context to it, one way or the other. As much as you might hear everything I've done so far and judge me for it, this was the first truly forward move I had made yet.

A moment later, two texts came in quick succession: ";)" and "Goodnight :)."

If you had messaged me and asked me at this point, I would have thought that things were going very, very well.

CHAPTER 8A

"Was that when you --" he asked, but was interrupted by the waitress. She was plump and had blonde hair with a pink streak in it, and was pretty when she smiled. He nodded at her and took his espresso, sipping it lightly. It was hot and stuck in the wisps of his facial hair. He did not finish the sentence once the waitress walked away.

Simon stared across the table at him. His own drink sat on the table in front of him, almost untouched, its dark liquid staining the pure white fabric of the cloth. The final remnants of the garlic bread he had been eating sat on the table next to it, bearing the marks of his teeth: one of the only things it was legitimately hard for him to fake for an extended period of time.

Slowly, he nodded.

CHAPTER NINE

Not long after that there was a late-night meeting at the office, with all senior staff and personnel in mandatory attendance. I was on that list and so was Craig -- and of course, so was Tyler Carter.

The reason for the meeting wasn't disclosed, even during its progress. Instead each team was given specific, even micro-managed tasks: correlating data from certain dates compared against other dates, finding productivity reports, seeing which accounts were outstanding and which were overdue, and – most importantly – seeing where fat could be trimmed. This resulted in catastrophic blitzkriegs of activity, followed by short lulls of refueling and coffee before another buzz of work.

Shane had military contracts -- and many of them -- in minor areas. Assembling nodes and complex circuits to be used in 'smart' weaponry. Programming. Simulations. All the work we were doing now rotated around these fields like planets around the sun, but did not touch them in any way. It drew my attention to them while trying to not draw my attention to them, like a murder suspect that goes too far out of his way to prove his innocence. We were filling this impromptu late-night with work that af-

fected our military division without specifically addressing it, at such a micro-managed level that no one person
had the chance to stop and look into that direction: there
was no spare second when one could branch from their
chosen task into the broader picture.

This meeting was announced in the morning, with no
warning, and we were prepared for the very likely event
that it would not be the last one of the week. As such, everyone looked tired, and I had to too. I pressed my thumbs
into my eyelids to make them as bloodshot as everyone
else's and reminded myself to get coffee every thirty minutes with begrudging movements. In truth, I needed very
little sleep: humans are more productive in the morning,
but since most people do not acknowledge this, network-
ing is done late at night. Having to do both, I've gotten
used to three-hours of sleep a night.

As a consultant my job – now – was largely to find
places where business could be made better. This was ideal
to my actual position, as I was afforded a greater glimpse
of the big picture. This included things like which departments solely existed to generate revenue with which to
fund certain other departments; which subsidiaries and
auxiliary companies were generating the most business,
and possibly why; and which patents paid off the greatest
licensing dividends.

It was a complex web that this largely public company
had created, and I passed many a tired, confused looking individual on my way to the kitchen for more coffee.
Many complained, without compunction, about how their
long hours at the office were affecting their home life.

That last complaint was the reason I was watching my

phone.

Every time I went to get a coffee or to the washroom, I would discover an opportunity to check my public-facing profile and see if I had received any recent calls or texts.

It was roughly eleven when I checked and saw that the text had come in. Two in fact, sent in rapid succession: "How is the meeting?" and "I'm bored."

It is a myth constructed by a mostly-male power structure in our society that most women who cheat do so out of boredom. This diminishes the act while simultaneously shifting the blame for the indiscretion solely onto the female partner. In truth, anything that happens in a relationship is the cause of something systemic within the relationship itself: poor communication, lack of agency, lack of urgency to find time for one another... any number of things. But 'bored' was the shorthand men of the business world have adapted: they're worried about leaving their wife home alone, and that she'll get bored and cheat. Not that they're emotionally unavailable, not that they've spent less time together than strangers, not that he is, in fact, cheating -- she's just bored. It's insulting.

But in an odd turn, the phrase has been "taken back" by women in a fashion similar to other phrases used to diminish the disenfranchised which I will not repeat here. "She's bored" when said *of* a woman is an insult to her intelligence and her virtue. "I'm bored" when said *by* a woman was using the male coded language for her own gain, to stealthily initiate their own agendas.

In this new arena, where language norms change constantly, "I'm bored" was the equivalent of texting "I'm horny," without bringing to mind a Michael Myers persona.

I was leaning against the wall in the hallway between the door to the kitchen and a small-framed picture of the ocean with the sun hanging over it, a city skyline only just visible in the foreground. The Shane main headquarters was there. It was titled "Los Angeles Sunrise". It was the type of commissioned art that businesses hung on the walls to try and appear friendlier, having been told that drab expressionless walls lead to suicides at time of stock dips.

I know that I was standing right there. It's one of those moments I remember with complete clarity: the people walking back and forth in front of me, getting their coffees. The smell of the brewer, arid and hot. The constant white noise of the murmur of conversations through walls. The fact that I had just missed something, and had not realized it. The smell of multiple perfumes and colognes and deodorants.

I answered back two quick texts: "That's a shame" and "A beautiful woman should never be bored."

If we're following the logic of what I'm saying 'bored' was code for, remind yourself of what I'm saying to her.

Several tense moments passed, and I imagined that I had gone too far. 'Beautiful' was by no means a salacious comment, but it was certainly an upgrade in intent from 'rare.' I thought I could afford to be more direct now: the baser one's instincts got, the less one was expected to show class. Nobody jumps into bed with their bow tie still on, and all that rubbish.

I was about to put my phone away again, when two more texts came: "I enjoyed our talk" and "I want to see you."

I looked around. I was exposed, but not in a way that anyone would recognize. Still, I became acutely aware suddenly that this woman's husband was in the same building as me, on the same floor.

"We can meet for coffee," I returned. I debated leaving a question mark by it, and decided not to. Statements were more forceful. The question still lingered from that first night, that very first interaction with her: what did she want me to be? Did she want me to be the hunter, seducing the boss's wife for the sport? Or did she want me to be the prey, victim of a stealthy lioness?

"We can," she responded. "But that's not what I said. ;)"

I paused, scrolling back up over the messages she'd sent, and trying to understand where I'd slipped. I like to think I would have gotten there eventually, but she didn't feel the need to afford me the time.

"I want to see you," she texted again. A moment later, a picture of her was on my screen. The current term is 'selfie', I believe. Her hair was done but loose and tumbled over her shoulders, her eyes locked onto the camera. She wore a black robe and red underwear and little else, the downward angle of the photograph affording a slanted angle down her cleavage.

At once, I understood.

"Now," she texted again, before I could respond to the photo.

Any question of whether she wanted me to be the hunter or the prey had vanished. I very suddenly knew my place, like a gazelle grazing on some grass in an open field before hearing an overturned rock or the snap of a twig. I couldn't have planned for this, but it couldn't have gone any better than what I'd planned. Things were happening at such a fast pace now; I could all but see the finish line. Months of planning and small pieces of puzzles, all falling into place.

"I'm at work right now, can't come out...;)" I responded. I debated purposely misspelling the word come, and decided against it. Too crass for this stage of the game.

"I know," she said quickly. "But that's not what I said. ;)"

The same phrase again. She was leading me and enjoying that she was leading me, enjoying the hunt in a way any good predator would. This was good: when the people whom you are conning take agency of their own actions and set off in the direction you led them into, it can be a very good thing. That is… if you set them off in the right direction... if I did my job right. The pieces I'd set in motion were now moving on their own, and that inertia would be hard to stop – perhaps impossible.

"You saw me, I want to see you... now. ;)"

The realization of what she meant hit me all at once, and I imagine the color drained from my face. This had escalated far too quickly, and I've come to believe that she knew that. Lydia was headed in the right direction all right, but faster than I could have anticipated. For the first time in what was now nineteen months, I must have been sweating.

"I'm at work ;)" I messaged back quickly. It hadn't had the wink at first, and I had added hastily before pressing send. I was trying to slow down this inertia, not stop it completely, and I was not so far down this road with Lydia that I didn't have to tread carefully.

"I've been there," she responded coyly. "I know they have broom closets. ;)"

Fuck.

I may have cursed out loud. I'm not sure. If I did, I hadn't ascribed any attention to myself.

I turned off my phone and quickly turned it back on, switching profiles. The new screen came up, the one without Lydia's texts, and I opened up the messenger app and texted seven words that I had never thought, even in my wildest imaginations, I would ever string together: "I need a picture of a penis."

There was a long, tense moment. I imagine that no matter what circumstances a text like that was received under it would always be surprising. A moment later I received: "... What?"

"Lydia."

"There's this thing, it's called 'The Internet'..."

I huffed, perhaps outwardly frustrated for the first time. I couldn't text Lydia from this profile, and for all I knew that situation was spiraling out of control while I tried to contain it here. "I can't take an image from Google," I sent, followed by: "Anything I can find quickly, she could also stumble upon."

"For fucks sake..." I received. Several tense moments later, a picture of a penis appeared in my messages. The photo was sharp and in focus, so much so that individual beads of sweat were distinguishable on it. It was held erect by the taker's thumb, rising up from a curly tuft of black pubic hair, brightly lit in the glare from the flash. I paused to realize how lucky I had been that the hair had not been blond.

Most importantly the background was dark enough that it could have been anywhere, including the broom closet of Shane San Diego, and I suspected that Lydia would not be subjecting the photo to rigorous forensic analysis to see what lay hidden in the shadows of the background.

I pressed my thumb hard against the image, sending it to my other profile.

"Thanks," I texted.

"The things I do for you..." was the response I got, before shutting off the phone and starting it back up again, in the 'Lydia-Facing' profile. Sure enough, the photograph – which I believe has the moniker 'dick pic,' much in the same way the photo Lydia took has been labelled a 'selfie' – was waiting for me in her message box. I pressed send, and it sent.

There was another understandably tense moment that followed, as the three small dots that indicated she was typing something appeared, then disappeared. Appeared, then disappeared. Finally, I got two responses back to back. The first comprised of three letters and an emoticon, the second of four letters and an emoticon: "Yum ;)" and "Ttyl ;)."

I think if I had been a betting man, 'yum' would have been the least likely response I would have placed money on... remembering of course that it wasn't *my* penis she was referring to, but another man's.

In any event, the situation with Lydia was escalating quickly. At this rate, it was conceivable that my deep cover would last less than twenty-one months, a full three months shorter than I had originally projected. Not that projections meant much in my line of work: it took as long as it took, and that was all there was to it.

There are things that happen when you are deep cover that you have to respond to that you couldn't possibly have accounted for. When preparing myself for activity nineteen months ago, there was no way I could have predicted that I would need a cache of genital photographs for use at a moment's notice, but those were the realities of deep cover: you could not accurately predict the needs of human behavior, in that exact a detail, over that long a timeframe.

"Hello, Simon," Tyler said happily as he stepped past me on his way to the washroom. He clapped me heartily on the shoulder as he stepped past, clearly on the upswing of a caffeine-induced high. I watched him go, this man whose wife I had just sent a picture of a penis to.

At that moment, I probably thought that things couldn't get any more complicated. I was very, very wrong about that.

I stepped into the kitchen to get a coffee.

CHAPTER TEN

The sad truth about deep cover is that things are going to get complicated, and the longer it goes on for the more likely that will be. On a long enough timeline, any situation ends in failure. That's not pessimism; it's just the truth.

I was pouring the rich black sludge from the bottom of a coffee pot into my cup when I felt something sharp poke me in the back, timed almost perfectly with a deadpan delivery of: "Simon."

I turned. Maggie was standing behind me.

My mistake hit me at once, as it would have had I not been so colossally drunk when I'd bumped into her at the bar. She'd said that she was "in accounting," which I had taken to mean, "I am in the profession of accounting..." What she had instead meant was, "I am in the accounting department."

Maggie worked with me.

Maggie knew me.

I feel as though my brain didn't function for several moments there, but I know there wasn't any of that. At least while I'm sober, I can manage to sustain a baseline ruse even on autopilot. "Hey," I smiled back. Was the smile forced? I'm not certain. I put down the pot of coffee and turned to face her and leaned against the counter of the break-room. I needed to think but there wasn't any time to think.

"How were you after?" she asked, beaming in a funny sort of way. She reached past me and picked up the pot herself, draining the last of the coffee into her cup. "I mean, clearly you survived."

I don't remember what I said. Have you ever had the experience of having someone from one part of your life intrude into another unwelcomed? Like having an ex-girlfriend start working at the same place you're currently working at, or something along those same levels? This felt like that, but worse. I felt my shoulders fall a little, the way they had that night at the bar. My posture changed, in a way that I was just perceptually aware of, and I had to concentrate to bring it back to the way I'd stood and walked for the last eighteen months. This was why you had to keep the same thoughts, the same demeanor, the same everything at all times when you were deep cover: stepping out of that bubble once made it only too easy to do so again.

Tyler walked by the kitchen, but didn't step in. Tyler knew Maggie, Maggie knew Tyler, and Maggie had met me. The real me, not the deep cover me.

"I watched *Prometheus* the other night on Netflix. I don't know what people were bitching about," she said. She brushed past me again – making contact and making no effort not to, grazing my arm. This conversation wasn't about movies; this was about the kiss. She had kissed me, right in the corner of my mouth, little sparks of electric heat between the night and us. That same part of my brain that had pinned down Lydia's intentions so well sprang to life and, without meaning to, without *wanting* to, I was reading her: the cut of her blouse, the shape of her hair, the angle of her body, the color of her nails and lipstick. She had wanted to bump into me tonight, on this late night at Shane San Diego, when everyone had to stay late until god-only-knew what hour.

She wasn't drinking her coffee. She had poured it, but she wasn't drinking it, and now she was sitting at the table in the center of the break room, her head facing me. This angled her legs toward the empty chair next to her: an open invitation. She wasn't drinking the coffee, and the cup she was holding had been clean. Was there a full cup back in her office, amidst a sea of revenue reports and TKS slips? Almost certainly. She'd kept a weather eye on the break room and had waited patiently, knowing that at some point during a long night, everyone had to refuel. Even track-star drama-geeks.

I told her that I hadn't seen the movie, but that I didn't think anything could top Ridley Scott's first *Alien* movie. She replied that Scott had actually returned to direct *Prometheus*. I conceded that I would have to check it out.

She lingered, her posture wavering. She didn't understand why I was different than I had been the other night -- more than just workplace professionalism or being sober versus being drunk, I was different now. Which made a lot of sense: I was looking for a way out now, whereas before I had been content to allow things to progress however they progressed. Now I was avoiding questions and taking part in the conversation just enough to shut it down, but doing so without being rude -- being rude could get around as well, and the last thing I wanted was to jeopardise the personae I had cultivated for a year and a half.

She paused after talking about the report she was working on, and I could watch her decide which way to press the conversation. She could give up or plunge forward. She teetered on the edge between one or the other for several seconds, her pupils dilating and pulse-rate quickening. "I think you should take me out to dinner," she said finally.

I raised an eyebrow at her. "Oh?" I asked quizzically. I knew why.

"To thank me for rescuing you the other night." Yes, that had been why. She got up then and stepped over to me, sliding her business card into my breast pocket. "I like Mexican," she said in a matter-of-fact tone, then turned and walked out of the room.

I had no idea whether Simon Monk liked Mexican or not, but it was looking more and more like I was going to have to find out.

CHAPTER ELEVEN

I broke three wine glasses the next day when I got home. There's something deeply satisfying about the way wine glasses specifically fall and crash; awkwardly weighted, falling end over end like some bizarrely drunken trapeze artist until finally: *crash*. Glass heads in one direction and the stem shatters down the center almost perfectly every time. Whenever I gathered up the shards, I gathered those stems – those shattered, phallic halves -- first even though they weren't sharp. I was careful with them even though they were not even remotely sharp.

Have you ever lost a train of thought and been unable to get it back? Experienced those frustrating, headache-inducing moments afterward when you search the nooks and crannies of your mind and the broken fragments of your concentration until you find yourself just exhausted? That's what it's like when deep cover gets broken, except instead of a train of thought, it's more like an identity. I had chosen to play the prey for Lydia, but was now juggling two women attached to the same office, a decidedly Hunter thing to do (not to speak ill of the dead). So which was I? Who was Simon Monk that he was both being chased by this older woman and (apparently) chasing Maggie? And for that matter, who had spread glass all over his kitchen floor? Was it Simon Monk or someone else entirely?

This was why you had to stay in-character at all times during a deep cover operation: because life wasn't divided into segments like an orange, clearly divided parts that you can separate and arrange onto separate plates. The different parts of life are more like the different strands of a cobweb, unable to be pulled apart and impossible to untangle.

Simon Monk had absolutely no reason to be breaking three cheap wine glasses all over his kitchen floor, because Simon Monk had no reason or right to be this upset that Maggie had asked him out, because Simon Monk had never *met* Maggie. Simon Monk had gone into that bathroom at the bar and not re-emerged into the land of the living until late the next morning. Some spectre had taken over his body and done things with it he never would have and didn't remember doing, and now he was faced with the consequences. Now he was faced with two choices: turn Maggie down and hope that it didn't get around the office and back to Tyler and, by extension, back to Lydia that Simon Monk was a bit of a cad, or go out with Maggie and hope that that information didn't follow the same path, also back to Lydia.

There was, of course, an option somewhere in the middle that I didn't even fully consider. I had narrowed down my options to a simple, binary damned-if-I-do and damned-if-I don't – because the truth of the matter was, even if Simon Monk hadn't had fun that evening at the bar, I had.

CHAPTER TWELVE

When I was in college, I dated two women who were roommates. I juggled them both for about a week and a half until it all came crumbling down around my ears and they both left me at the same time, in a rather spectacular fashion. It was possibly my first experience with the pitfalls of living a double life, but more than that, it was one of my first experiences with compartmentalization. The fact was it never once occurred to me that I was doing something wrong until they confronted me. I legitimately felt horrible when I realized the truth. When I was with Betty, I really liked Betty and didn't think of Veronica much. When I was with Veronica, I didn't think of Betty much. I wasn't trying to be nefarious or anything.

No, those weren't their names; those are fictional characters and a part of Americana pop culture.

As much as I tried to tell myself differently, this wasn't that. Compartmentalization is an important part of deep cover, but Maggie was a part of both compartments. She knew Craig, or at least knew of him.

The only solution I could think of, then, was to move up the timeline of the Lydia situation. It was a risk certainly, but not as much as allowing these two systems to interact side-by-side was, as any chemist worth his salt will tell you.

I sat on my hands for seven agonizing days, afraid to make a move in either direction for fear of upsetting the delicate homeostasis that had been obtained.

When there was another late night at the office to go over the files and reports from the last quarter, I called in and let them know that I was going to be staying home sick. Tyler Carter called me back himself to make sure I was alright and to ask if there was anything he could do. I told him it was just a twenty-four hour bug and that I didn't want to give it to the rest of the staff, as busy as we were. He thanked me and told me to take the next day as well. I almost felt bad. If this level of trust hadn't been exactly what I had been working toward for almost nineteen months, I think I would have.

As soon as I hung up with Tyler, I opened up my text messaging and texted Lydia: "I'm not going in to the office tonight."

The message I got back did not contain any words, only a map reference to her home.

As though I hadn't known exactly where she'd lived for months.

CHAPTER THIRTEEN

Lydia and Tyler's home was beautiful, of the sort that people like you and I only dream about after seeing them on television. It was modelled after Victorian houses and had one of those massive spiralling staircases with every step ivory white and the size of my bed in college. There was a chandelier at the cusp of the staircase that hung down in a glistening crystal V-shape -- the shape of a womb. That's the difference between people pretending to be rich and people who are actually rich, you know: people who pretend to be rich cultivate things shaped like a phallus to overcompensate for their perceived inadequacy for not being truly rich. Those with real wealth didn't feel the need to prove anything, and as a result most things had the cupped, V-shape of a rudimentary womb.

I entered just after I knocked, not waiting for her to answer or acknowledge or even make sure I had the right house. I knew I had the right house, of course -- had discovered it before I'd even started my deep cover. That was where I had first seen Lydia Carter, sunning herself on her front yard when the Google van had come along to snap a picture of her property for Street-View. She'd been wearing a white two-piece and those big round sunglasses that only beautiful women can get away with wearing, her lips a small red smear beneath them. A bottle of lemonade sat on the grass next to her sun chair, a pink crazy straw sticking out of it lazily as condensation ran down the outside of the bottle. The entire picture looked hot. It looked like summer. She looked like an older woman -- not in the sense of what it means to me now, but what it had meant to me then: childhood summers spent mowing lawns for change under that watchful gaze of Megan Vance's mother, who in my teenage years was an 'older woman' at thirty-four. Those pictures, with the green of the grass and the white of her swimsuit and the red of her lipstick and the lens flare -- those pictures ignited the unrequited awe that comes only with early adolescence.

I entered just after I knocked, not waiting for her to answer, the ultimate display of ownership. I was entering the home of another man to bed his wife and I acted as though I belonged. I did not wait to be allowed in, to be led around and shown each room with passing interest ("Here is the living room." "Oh?" "Here is the kitchen."); I stepped in as though it, and she, were already mine to have.

She was standing halfway up those spiral stairs, white satin kissing her and hanging from her and dangling to just barely expose bare feet. She had not been in mid-motion, as though I had caught her coming down the stairs to meet me or do some chore. She had been standing there, her hair up and her eyes hungering for me, as though she had known I would enter of my own accord.

I maintained my eye contact with her as I shut the door behind me. For a long moment the air between us was tense, with neither of us knowing exactly what to say. Except that I did know what to say, and I knew exactly how long to wait before saying it. I knew how long to let the tension sit and let the heat between us build, separated by nothing but ten feet of open air for the first time since the Christmas party.

There's something about that moment that makes it the best moment in any relationship. That tense excitement when both parties feel as though there is no turning back from what will happen, but before it has actually begun to happen. That electricity is rare and only happens when it's new and so precious.

For a moment I envied her, because she alone was experiencing that jolt.

After I've waited what I knew was the appropriate amount of time, I smirked at her out of one side of my mouth and pushed my thumb back towards the door, and said, "It was open."

She smiled and laughed and came the rest of the way down the stairs, reaching out her hand to lead me into the sitting room.

Sexual encounters of this kind count among the most riveting games of chess on the planet. There's something about that sort of good strategy that just aches of pleasurable tension and makes it a universal human experience, as cathartic as the event itself. Both of us knew why we were there and both of us were there for that only reason, and yet the process of getting to that was better than the act itself. Curious, no?

We sat on a couch whose back leaned back in front of a roaring fire, the light from the dancing flames making her glow. She looked young, with the orange ambiance on her pale flesh and the white of her eyes, leaning against the back of the couch and facing me in a position reminiscent of the shape a woman takes when laying next to the welcome open area of a bed.

She handed me a drink and at first I was hesitant – not that I thought she would drug me or hamstring me, you understand, but because I did not want a repeat of the incident at Theories. I took it tentatively, holding it by the base so that I could smell the sweet scent of it. There were hints of plum and citrus and just this small, small hint of chocolate. I cannot emphasize enough how slight this hint of chocolate was, almost unidentifiable but just enough to tease at my frontal lobe and send a jolt through it. It was enough to take me by surprise, and I went back for another, longer smell, following up my "Hello there" with a longer "I'm fine thanks, and you?" to misquote Richard Paterson. I finally took a sip and let it rest on my tongue. "Walker?"

"Eighteen year," she smiled. She had been watching me enjoy the drink with rapt fascination. The care at which I took to fully enjoy it was metaphor for her expectations of my sexual prowess. All food and drink was metaphor for sex when sex was what one really wanted the taste of. I should have seen it back at the Christmas party in the way she watched me devour those tiny hors d'oeuvres: oral fixation, without a doubt.

I regarded the glass with some respect and took another drink. "It's been a while since I had something eighteen year," I said as I laid it down and turned back toward her. "I typically prefer something a little older on my tongue."

She laughed, and not the way I'd heard her laugh before. The laugh was honest, but at the same time held intent. She took her hand away from her cheek and pressed it to mine, touching it with the sort of deft feathery touch that I will never be able to accomplish. My hands are only capable of determined, punctuated motions. Hers moved on the breeze and caressed with the fleetingness of pure silk.

She reached for her own glass, and I took measure of it: scotch, the same amount and likely the same brand as mine. They had been laid down before I got here and hers may have been watered down. Discounting the first glass then, I would have to watch my intake carefully to remain in control above and beyond her.

She allowed her laugh to trail off into a hum; the way women on television do to let you know that they were laughing at the sexual joke you just made -- not to undercut it, but to affirm it. I say 'women on television' because I have never seen a woman I was in a real relationship with do that. It is a pattern of behavior exclusive to women of television shows, extramarital affairs, and one-night stands. Perhaps when we are not at our most comfortable we revert to the personality tropes society has taught us, and since the late 1950s, society has done its teaching through an idiot box filled with actors not good enough for film. She returned to the couch with a flop, the sort of fun and relaxed motion of those truly enjoying themselves. I think if I weren't me, I would look back on that moment with some guilt. She was beginning to relax, the firelight touching her like soft gauze and making her into a sepia-toned memory. With one pull of something that I hadn't noticed before and which disappeared immediately afterward, her hair was down and in luscious bobbing curls around her bare shoulders.

"What have you been keeping yourself occupied with?" she asked, taking a healthy drink from her glass.

I smiled. "Work, mostly. And school."

"School?"

"Yes," I said, a lie. "I teach a culinary class at the New School on Harvey Crescent." Another lie. "I'm also taking an intro course in fine art." Another lie. "The School lets instructors take classes for free." Possibly a lie, possibly the truth. I didn't fact check it. I know some better universities have such a program. "I try and take something new every term." Elaboration on a lie. "It broadens my horizons." Technically this would have been true if the classes were true, but they weren't so: lie. "Last semester I took anthropology." Such a lie. You know that one was a lie.

With every point I made, her head moved and twitched in that sweet, attentive way. She never broke eye contact, except to get more of her drink and to look at my mouth. I think she liked watching me talk in equal parts because of what I was saying and because she liked watching my mouth at work.

Oral fixation confirmed. I was almost insulted; I had spent the better part of a week researching her on social media and tailoring the perfect background for myself that would complement the gaps in my deep cover, and here she was more interested in the double-kiss my lips made when I said 'New School.' Whatever small part of me was insulted (likely none) was at the same time flattered by the attention though. I'm never arrogant enough to assume I'm attractive, but every so often when it's confirmed that I am (at least in the eyes of some), I wonder if all my pre-planning and memorization is necessary. Perhaps I could just walk in and bat my eyelashes and be done with it. The world will never know.

Her eyes were hungry and drank me in. I tried to lose myself in the moment almost entirely; some things cannot be faked. As I've said before, compartmentalization is a key part of deep cover. 99.9% of my brain was right here in the role of the salacious youth putting the moves on the boss's wife. Only that remaining 0.1% was monitoring the amount of alcohol I was sipping and making sure I pronounced words like 'mobile' correctly.

The firelight was on her skin and she looked too soft to be real. Her fingertips were grazing the edges of the straps on her shoulders, not moving them but teasing them, reminding me how little effort it would take to make them fall away. Her every gesture and look and smell was an invitation. She took another drink from her glass, finishing it. As she placed it back, I moved forward, completely in the moment, as one must be in times like this. There are some things that cannot be faked no matter how many months one has been in deep cover.

The air was thick between us. Closing the distance between our bodies was like swimming through warm, smooth gelatin. She closed her eyes just as they're lost in my peripheral vision, the first respite she'd given me from her hypnotic gaze since I entered. An instant later our lips met, our mouths open only slightly and then widening as we sank into the kiss, warm and smooth and just right.

Her mouth was tiny, I realized, as I took her cheek into the cup of my hand.

Maggie.

The thought came to me from nowhere. The 99.9% didn't know Maggie -- it had been involved in a sordid affair with Lydia Carter for over a month. The 0.1% had been busy with my accent and alcohol and basic bodily functions. Now my eyes were open as the image of Maggie standing in front of me as she waited to get her cab, just before she leaned forward and kissed me, was in my head. All 100% of my brain was screaming red flashing cherry lights and clanging whooping alarms, convinced that this thought has come from some heretofore unknown portion of my mind: a secret percent that had until now been hidden, the grand total actually being 101%, the remaining one a vestige of evolution long thought deserted with Darwin's beaks.

I felt her hands on the back of my neck, lightly dancing fingernails, and hoped she didn't notice. Our bodies were pressed together, warmth meeting warmth. The only sound was the fire and our lips and she tasted and smelled of the same dark chocolate aroma that had been in the Scotch. At once, the 99.9% kicked back in and the kiss was almost all I'm doing again, my autonomous sensory meridian response sending gooseflesh all down my arms.

Maggie came to mind again, across from me at Theories and plopping complimentary peanuts on her upper lip before swallowing them.

I moved slightly, shaking her (and the alarms in my head) away. The motion was noticed by Lydia this time and the kiss ended, though gently and not abruptly.

"Mmm," she smiled as we parted, resting her head on her arm. In her youth, she would have said added wow to the end, but we're both far too old for such games. Neither of us would be the best the other has ever had, but we were both long past the notion that an act must top all others in order to be enjoyable. Our lips met again briefly as I leaned back and we both smiled; I hoped mine looked natural.

I wanted to ask the question, but we weren't there yet. Head-rush dulls the facilities quite a bit, but not enough that the wrong thought at the wrong time cannot snap one to attention. I glanced at her empty glass; mine was still three quarters full. I picked up mine with my right hand, obscuring its contents, and grabbed hers as well. "I'll refill."

She nodded, playing with her hair.

I walked to the bar and confirmed the bottle is Jonny Walker, aged eighteen years. I remember a time when I would have drank anything: pink sludge purloined from a parent's liquor cabinet with floating balls of gelatin in it, tasting of cranberries and shame. The memory came to me like something out of another life and almost set my pulse on fire, but I managed to stay calm. Where had it come from? And those thoughts of Maggie; why did they keep intruding? Where were they coming from, what forgotten corner of my misbehaving brain?

I mimed pouring myself some more Johnny Walker, and then did pour myself some more cola to water down what remained in my glass. It would taste like filth, but sacrifices had to be made. I poured Lydia two fingers and then a splash more for luck and topped it with just enough cola to change the color, not bringing it to the brim.

Advantage had to be gained somewhere, especially when it seemed part of my own mind was out to get me.

CHAPTER 13A

Simon bit into his steak and moisture came out of it in succulent driblets. He chewed, looking down at the untouched salad on the side of his plate – a strawberry spinach concoction with dried almonds and red wine reduction – as he chewed. Once he swallowed, he looked up and realized that the man sitting across from him was shuffling uncomfortably. "What?"

"Getting a woman drunk?"

Simon rolled his eyes. "May I remind you I was doing it to avoid taking advantage of her?"

The man's eyelids bobbed, but he said nothing.

Simon took another bite of his steak.

CHAPTER FOURTEEN

There were several more drinks. I even had another non-virginal scotch and soda, poured myself to make sure it wasn't as full as the last. In many ways, it was the best sort of foreplay -- both parties knowing that the other wanted something from them, both wanting to come out on top and gain some edge on the other. I've always found that casual sex is at its best when adversarial... I'm not saying I like that truth or what it says about society or gender relations or sexual politics, it's just what I happen to have found to be the truth.

There were several more drinks and a lot more kissing, hot and sweet with the residue of the alcohol and cola on our lips. At one point, I was nuzzled in the nape of her neck for what felt like forever, suckling on the tender flesh I found there. It was one of the only times I lost myself in the action of the role, without thinking about what I was supposed to be doing or about Maggie or Tyler. There was something about the nape of a good woman's neck I've always found particularly appealing; I believe it has something to do with the fact that it's one of the key positions for depositing perfume. Whatever the reason, it was intoxicating.

There was conversation too. Those are the things they always leave out of the movies -- you know the ones. The spy and the girl go right to bed and the audience is left wondering how that even happens. While this type of encounter does happen, it often leads to the sort of awkward "putting on the clothes while avoiding eye contact" type of conversation after the fact that all parties hope to avoid. No, successful affairs can be some of the only times when adults have good, fulfilling conversations. You already know that the evening will end in sex, so you can be perfectly candid, and since there's a certain level of secrecy involved in the whole endeavor, you know that your words will be kept. It's like having a therapist you can go to bed with. Or in my case, *being* a therapist you can go to bed with, as I let her do most of the talking.

She told me about her childhood growing up in Algeria, her parents having been professionals working there with the UN at the time. She spoke of large stone cities built into the stone face of the earth until one was indistinguishable from the other, deserts that stretched so far that a child could become convinced that they encompassed the entire planet, lush greenery the likes that put the color in America to shame, and palaces that made one dream of being a princess as though it could be true. She told me about not wanting to leave when she was ten, but having to anyway, and of the culture shock of coming back to America and being surrounded on all sides by whites.

She told me about her first crush, a young boy named David Elgee who lived three houses down from her when she was twelve years old. He'd had blond hair and blue eyes and in her memory always wore horizontal-striped t-shirts as though he had stepped straight out of a sepia-toned photograph from the 1950s. He worked in Santa Cruz now, she said; she'd looked him up on social media.

The wonders of modern technology.

She told me about her first time, the sort of sordid hot affair in her parents' garage while they were still at home in the house: no time to be fancy, only the time to make it happen, the sort of quick, insane lovemaking that only children can do. She had been fifteen, which had at the time seemed impossibly old to be a virgin and now seemed impossibly young to not be.

As she told me this last story, I had become nuzzled in her neck and had perhaps faintly fondled her breasts, and may have missed some of the finer details. If she noticed, she did not seem particularly upset by this.

As I took my lips away from her neck, she caught them with her mouth and pulled me in with them; her lips grabbed me with sheer force that couldn't have been broken if I'd tried. Her legs were around me, the heels of her small feet pressing into the small of my back and pressing me close to her. She rocked me against her, grinding against me, her hands cupping the sides of my face and grazing the short hairs on the back of my head.

She was an intoxicating woman. When I tell people that I had to sleep with an older woman for the job, they picture some overweight behemoth with which I did the job for the sake of the job: this was not Lydia in any sense. This was not doing a woman I found distasteful for the purpose of a job I enjoyed; this was being unable to enjoy a woman because of a job I found distasteful.

The blood tried to rush from my head and I tried hard

to keep it there, calculating my level of drunkenness: 3 – 1 – 1 + 1 = 2. Two was not bad; at two I could still make logical choices and sense cues and meanings in subtext with enough virility to act on them accordingly in verbal chess.

Lydia was 3 + 2 + 2 + 1 making her an eight, easily. Lydia was drunk, on the level that while she likely still wouldn't do things she wouldn't have wanted to, she was more apt to say things she wouldn't have meant to. She'd also had twelve fluid ounces of an eighteen-year-old depressant in her system in the last seventy minutes, which also worked well into my long-term goals. I estimated her weight at 120 pounds... she should have had a blood-alcohol level of 0.14, but was exhibiting signs of the 0.16 that I needed her to be at: the sort of sloppy drunk where social drinkers begin to feel incapacitated.

I do realize how this sounds, yes.

She must have had a drink before I'd arrived.

I felt her hand leave my face and slide its way down to my fulcrum. She gripped hungrily and urgently at the one thing I could not be disingenuous of. I took her hand away was a strong grip, lacing our fingers together and holding her hand above her head with force. She moved pleasingly beneath me despite this, her other hand still on the back of my neck. It took hold of my head by the ear and pulled to one side, bringing her lips to my neck and then breaking away as she gasped for air.

"Take me to the bedroom," she said, her mouth open and sensual.

I pause. For the act, this is for dramatic affect and to make sure she is sure. In reality, I am making last minute calculations, trying my best to decide whether or not she had had that crucial extra beverage. 0.16. 120 pounds. Twelve ounces.

It was time.

"What if Tyler comes home?" I asked, the first time I had dared to say his name.

She smiled sensually, her fingernails running up and down my neck. Her smile found me adorable, cute, like a boy anxious to get caught. "Tyler won't be coming home."

I smiled and took her into my arms, lifting her effortlessly. I realized at once I may have been slightly generous with the 120 estimate: we were at 0.16, I was sure of it. She made long, loud 'wooop' sound and then laughed as I hopped over the couch with her and back out into the parlor where we had begun and began ascending the stairs two at a time. She pulled my head to hers and we kissed, her teeth catching at my lip and pulling me in and forcing me out all at the same time.

I'm not sure how I made it to her bedroom with our faces locked in struggle that way, but I made it as though we'd done this hundreds of time before. I tossed her onto the bed and she bounced and laughed, and a moment later I was on her and my hands were everywhere at once: first in her hair and then on her face and then at her breasts and finally engrossed in the deep warmth where her legs met. We moved back tond forth, rocking and kissing and locking eyes when we were not kissing. She grabbed my face with surprising strength, her fingers fanned like starfish on either side of my head as her body arched and angled against mine, her eyes never leaving mine even as the sounds of my bringing her to climax rang in my ears.

Without a pause, my hands slipped past her undergarments and slid them away, then turning to the warm, wet cleft framed by the wispy hints of pubic hair. She was like silk beneath me and I could see the surprise in her as I brought her immediately the downward direction of one orgasm into the upward climb toward another.

She reached for my trousers – pants, sorry – and began to unbutton them.

This was it. This was the real show. I didn't tell you about what I did with her to be vulgar -- deep cover necessitates you be well versed in a good many things and this was one of them. There was the setup, the promise of more, and then there was the 0.16 -- the thing that would make what came next possible and facilitate my getaway.

I brought my hand gently to hers as it unzipped me. I carefully made sure my voice had lost all machismo and that my eyebrows were upturned and innocent: "Are you *sure* Tyler won't come home?"

She laughed and kissed me. "My darling, Tyler won't be home all night... he practically sleeps at the office getting ready for the merger."

DING DING DING DING DING

We have a winner. There was going to be a merger. And now, knowing that, of *course* there was going to be a merger. A merger from which Shane would not emerge the controlling interest by a generous margin. A merger so secretive that only individual heads knew, no employees at any level, and investigations into finances had to be carried out under a vial of secrecy and lies.

I had brought Lydia Carter to climax after seventy

minutes of anticipation and she had almost gone insane with it. My release came after almost twenty months of deep cover, and the sense of ease that followed was just as exponentially great.

I could take no time to celebrate. I brought my mouth down to her stomach and Lydia let her head fall back onto the soft down pillow behind her, her eyes rolling back into her head with anticipation renewed. I slid her dress up past her knees and thighs, exposing the milky flesh of her. Her hands touched the sides of my head, but after a moment fell to her side.

I kissed my way up to her breasts and then down to her stomach again, not striking her or paying any more attention to the fire in the joint of her legs. She moaned, softly, as I did this, avoided the areolas, remaining for a moment, then slowly and gently making my way back to her stomach.

Being bad in bed is as much a skill as being good in bed. Men brag about being good in bed, and I maintain I did not tell you about what happened above with the intent of bragging: exciting Lydia Carter then was as equally important as this was now. Men who brag about being good in bed neglect to realize that procreation hinges on our enjoyment of sex: we are made to enjoy it, our body tries hard to enjoy it, bringing blood to all the right places. One has to try quite methodically to not be arousing to a woman... to be downright boring. To be such that the weight of the pillows and the down sheets around you and the 0.16 blood-alcohol level in your blood suddenly has more urgency than the throb in your loins.

I kissed Lydia one last time and stood up, knowing

full well by the steadiness of her breathing that she had fallen asleep.

I buttoned myself back up and made for the door, then stopped, went back, and placed an afghan around her up to her shoulders.

As I exited the Carter residence, Maggie was only on the peripherals of my mind. It had been the first time that night that my mind had not been screaming her name. The majority of my mind was alive with one thought and one thought only:

Merger.

CHAPTER FIFTEEN

Over the course of the next week, I sent a total of three texts comprised of that word and nothing else:

Merger.

Such a simple word, isn't it? Get one word in your train of thought long enough and it will start to lose all meaning, to the point that you have to start reminding yourself of that meaning. "Merger: a combination of two things, especially companies, into one." 'Especially companies': right there in the definition.

Do you have any interest in etymology? It's odd how many imperative words have single-syllables while two-syllable words are often much more... sinister. Single-syllable words include gun, food, drink. Double includes murder, merger, killer. When I was young I knew a ghost-writer who said he chose the names of his villains based on the two-syllable rule -- except that I didn't know him, Simon Monk knew him. And Simon Monk was a reality that was not only coming apart but was quickly proving itself unnecessary.

And yet, there was Maggie. That *other* two-syllable name.

Aside from the three single-word text messages I

sent that week, I had had one awkward "post-coital" text conversation with Lydia; her 0.16 BAC appeared to have done the trick as intended. She neither had any memory of mentioning the merger, nor was she aware that we had *not* had intercourse. She assumed that we had continued and that she had lapsed in memory due to the drink. This wasn't ideal, but was better than the alternative. I had also had two brief textual interactions with Maggie: she asked me if I knew of any good Mexican restaurants; I told her The Pepper was good. She asked if I had had any plans that night; the answer was no.

By the time Friday rolled around again, I was sitting at my desk at Shane scrolling through these four messages, each set a day apart. I was thumbing the touch-screen on my phone to scroll them up and down even though all four lines of text were visible on one screen, the words bouncing uselessly against the top or bottom of the page with each flick of my digit.

Knowing that there would be a merger was not enough. It was something, but it wasn't enough. Knowing that there was going to be a merger would be enough to plummet Shane stock and certainly get Tyler Carter fired if either of those things had been my intention, and certainly if the information were to become public. A great deal of money could be made with the inside information during trading, again if that had been the intent. Neither was. For our intentions, it wasn't enough that there was to be a merger, it had to be known whom it was *with*.

For a week I had combed through any information I could without drawing suspicion: TPS reports, business trips (who, where, and for how long), meal receipts, and hotel bills. Were there adult movies ordered during the night at the hotel? Then he didn't actually stay at the hotel, it was a front. On Wednesday Tyler came to check on me, to make sure I wasn't working myself too hard to make up for the sick day I'd taken. I'd smiled and said I wasn't, that I felt fine, and shook his hand while some small hidden part of me chuckled with forced puritan awkwardness.

I received the documents from Accounting via courier.

As a general rule that was a bad idea. The more people involved in the actions of a deep cover, the harder it gets to maintain. Many hands do not make for light work in the realm of deep cover. It would have been far better for me to go down to Accounting myself to retrieve the records -- and yet I could not bring myself to do so.

What was happening? How I had I allowed everything to become so... un-compartmentalized? Despite all my efforts to the contrary, Maggie bled into all aspect of my cover. I would need to do the majority of my investigation in Accounting, which I was now avoiding like the plague. At the same time, any attempt to text her and honor our date for Mexican food (still necessary at this point for maintaining cover, above all else) was met with the brick wall of Lydia: I could see her face, held between my hands, and it left pangs in me. Was it guilt over betraying Lydia? No. I owed her nothing.

Maggie refused to stay in the box my mind had made from her, and nature abhors a vacuum, so the contents of the boxes she infested in to fill the gap. She was in everything and everything was in her, to my great frustration.

There had been a PDF detailing project headings for

the last twelve months open on my desktop for fifteen minutes without my eyes glancing toward it. Craig had provided it without so much as a second thought, but instead of reading it, my thumb flicked the corner of my smartphone screen, making those four lines of dialog between Maggie and I bounce and twitter.

In one movement, in one of those moments when we act without fully aware of what we are doing, I turned off the computer screen and typed, "let's have dinner" and hit send.

CHAPTER SIXTEEN

We didn't go out to The Pepper. Apparently I didn't know anything about Mexican food, but that was okay, she was going to show me.

"As a rule of thumb," she said, wrinkling her button nose at me, "don't expect any good Mexican food from a Mexican restaurant with an Anglo name."

This was a good rule of thumb, and for the first time in years I did not file it away under compartment X or Y for later use, I just laughed and agreed that that was likely true.

We went to Capistrano, a small place downtown that had been made out of a converted home. The building still looked like a home in the front face, except for the neon sign that cycled the letters O – P – E – N in second-long intervals. Inside it was the heart of kitsch, the flaking paint the rust red of dried adobe and dollar-store framed pictures of quasi-Mexican art on the walls.

"That's the other thing," she said as she sat down opposite me in a small booth in the corner. She pointed to a print of an orange-skinned man with a wide face hefting a large knapsack filled with corn. "If there's good art, it's not a good Mexican restaurant. Real Mexican restaurants are too busy giving a shit about the food to give a shit about what's on the walls."

I laughed again. "There is no art on the wall at The Pepper. It's very chic, very modern. The walls are all this glossy white, I think they're paneled in plastic."

She raised an eyebrow at me. "Are you sure this wasn't an Apple store?"

We both laughed. As it trailed off, I cleared my throat, looking around absently. "How have the late nights in Accounting been treating you?"

"Mmm," she hummed, taking a sip of her water. "Uh-uh. No. No work please. That's what made our night out at the bar so great: there was no work talk."

She didn't know how true that was.

"What did you do this week that wasn't work?"

I stared at her for what felt like an eternity. Lying has to be second nature in deep cover; that is the *point* of deep cover. The answer has to just be on the tip of your tongue, as easily as the truth would be. Now ten different things that Simon Monk had done or would have done in his off time flashed through my mind, none of which I had actually done. Even if I had done them, they would have not been answers to her questions -- Simon Monk's leisure activities were still a part of my workweek. "... Nothing," I said finally, after far too long a pause.

She laughed, glancing my hand with her own. "I... had a bit of an RDJ marathon."

"RDJ?"

"Robert Downey Junior," she smiled. "It started out just watching *Bowfinger* because *Bowfinger* is one of those movies I watch every three years or so for no reason at all.

It's like I have a little alarm clock inside me that somebody wound up and it goes off every so often and reminds me to watch *Bowfinger*. Weird, right?"

I nodded, and felt myself shifting and getting more comfortable. I was watching her talk. And not in some bored, un-fascinated way -- I was genuinely interested in not only what she was saying, but *how* she was saying it: the shape her lips made when she said the word *Bow*, curling like the word itself. The way her hair tickled the edges of her face when she laughed. Just how big her eyes were, and the way her cheeks pushed up into their territory when she smiled. I was watching it all, rapt.

"Then I had to watch *Kiss Kiss Bang Bang*, have you seen it? Amazing movie. It's almost a deconstruction of a movie; the way Harry – that's Robert Downey's character – keeps addressing the audience in his narration and breaking the movie down. It's like it's aware it is a movie, or at the very least aware that it's a story that's being told. Really he plays two characters, Harry and the Narrator, because the Harry we see and the one the Narrator talks about aren't totally the same person. What's that called?"

"An unreliable narrator?"

"Unreliable narrator," she nodded, snapping her fingers. "So by this point I'm in full RDJ mode. Twice is a coincidence; three times is a pattern. So I break out *The Singing Detective* with a bottle of red wine and some cheese on cheap crackers."

"Naturally," I laugh.

"The next night I hit up *A Scanner Darkly*. I read every Phillip K Dick novel I could get my hands on in college after this one prof made us read *Do Androids Dream of Electric Sheep* and watch *Bladerunner*. Loved the book, movie was okay. Not the point. Next was *Good Night, and Good Luck.* -- and I know I'm not going in any way close to chronological order here, but who cares."

"Now I've seen *Good Night, and Good Luck.*," I said, raising my finger.

"Really? Not one of the better-known," she smiled. "What'd you think?"

"Loved the rhetoric. And just the whole examination of McCarthyism. Something about the news media back then, really taking on the estate... never happens today."

Maggie nodded enthusiastically.

I *had* watched *Good Night, and Good Luck.*, many times. Almost fifty times in the run of a week in fact. I had used it at one point to get a certain annunciation and affectation down pat... but I'd enjoyed it so much, I had put it on once or twice since when not in deep cover, even though I always inadvertently defaulted to examining how David Strathairn said the word 'can't' after a few minutes.

... was there anything left in my life I allowed myself to just enjoy?

"So I go from *Good Night, and Good Luck.* to *Zodiac*, and I think there's a certain logical leap there. Then I watched *The Judge* and then last night I watched *Chaplin*. I think I like him best when he's playing real people... or, roles based on real people... you get me."

It was a statement, not a question. I *did* get her. And on the tail end of this revelation, came another... why did this incredible woman even like me as it seemed she did? She said it herself, she preferred when the actor played roles based on real people, which I was not. Simon Monk

was a fabrication, not some historically forgotten journal-
ist. There had never been a man that had to waltz around
town with a button that said, 'I am not Simon Monk' on
his breast.

I shook the thought away. Where had this anxiety
come from? I picked up the menu, but found that it was
only a drink menu.

Her smile slowly grew as she watched the puzzled ex-
pression on my face, the straw of her drink lingering near
her small mouth. "Real Mexican restaurants don't have
menus either," she hummed when she finally thought I
had suffered enough.

I raised an eyebrow at her just as the server walked
over. She looked up at him, exposing her slender white
neck, and in an instant any thought of question or anxiety
was gone. All thought was gone, actually, except those of
that thin line of flesh, the mouth they led to, and the scent
of the perfume on it.

"Aguachile with bolillo to start," she said, her tongue
rolling over the syllables as though it were her native one.
"Then flauta, chicken and beef, with jicama. Fresh if you
have it please." The waiter nodded once and stepped away
without writing anything down, and she turned back to
me and rested her chin on entwined fingers.

I paused a moment, then laughed. "You needed to
know a good Mexican restaurant?"

She laughed as well, adjusting her straw again, then
shook her head and smiled. "That's adorable."

I stopped, smiling. "What is?"

"After you laugh, sometimes you say words with an
accent. It's too cute."

CHAPTER SEVENTEEN

All of the food was sharable, all on one big plate between us. Our fingers touched often, sending sparks of electricity up my arm. Eventually we got used to it, and then we got comfortable with it, and then it became a sort of game with the food as tokens: I would reach for a piece of food and she would grab it, and vice versa. I took one succulent piece of flatbread with green salsa the consistency of silly putty from her and then offered it back to her. She opened her mouth and I put it in, the hand that was under it to stop any droppings catching the smooth skin of her chin. When she closed her mouth, it was millimeters from my thumb, and rarely had so small a distance seemed so important.

The appetiser was salty, succulent shrimp sautéed with chilli peppers and lime and coriander and thick slices of fresh red onion. There were fresh cucumbers on the side that were the only salve to my burning taste buds and I brought the mixture to my lips more and more readily, the spice only bearable in the moment the tasty seafood was first placed on the tongue. It was served with savory bread in the shape of an oval with a crunchy exterior and soft interior that felt good in the mouth. It was still warm, freshly baked.

The main course was rolled tortillas packed tight with chicken and beef and dipped in beans and sour cream and a yam blend that I learned from Maggie was the mysterious jicama that she had requested be as fresh as possible. She continued to eat this even after I considered it gone, collecting the last remnants on her small finger and then placing it in her mouth.

The food was good. The company was better.

Simon Monk did not eat like this. Simon Monk stuck to foods that kept him regular and out of gastric distress, because one did not know what the next day or even the next hour would bring. Simon Monk also did not shoot tequila for desert, but I did that too.

I walked her home. It was a long walk, but neither of us questioned it.

We talked about politics but about nothing particularly political. We laughed at a violinist still performing on the street and talked about music and got into a heated discussion about the films of Quinton Tarantino. We stopped at a small shop and got gelato in cones made in-house by a baker that knew her by name and spoke it with an elongated 'ie'. We sat on a park bench, not because we were tired but because it seemed like an unspoken thing to do -- neither of us suggested it, we both just did it. She sat close to me, my right side pressed tight to her left in the night air.

When we reached her front door, I did not ask to come in. I said goodnight and smiled at her. She jolted in as she had the night at Theories and kissed me, lightly on the lips.

As she was pulling back, I took her face in my hands and found her lips again, as well as her tongue.

It may have been the most perfect single kiss of my adult life, of the sort that we look back upon nostalgically and without regret.

We said goodnight and I stayed on her stoop until she was inside, then walked back to Capistrano to retrieve my car, feeling as though my feet did not touch the ground once the entire time.

CHAPTER EIGHTEEN

There was this kid in IT Craig had introduced to me a month before, named Nelson. He was the young bookish type; you know the kind. One can't blame Hollywood for perpetuating the stereotype of the bespectacled social misfit in that role if reality keeps doing it for its own casting calls as well.

"Look harder," I said. My arms were folded across my chest and I stared at his screen over his shoulder. "There are files missing from R&D and Marketing. They were there when I did my audit and now they aren't; what happened to them?"

Nelson shrugged in that non-committal way fifteen year olds often do, though he was twenty-seven. "They're just gone."

I frowned deeply. "Nothing is ever gone on a Windows server. Not that quickly at any rate. That's why we destroy hard drives with a hammer before they go out the door to the dump. If you know what you're doing, just about anything can be recovered."

He turned slightly and looked at me over his shoulder. I straightened -- Simon Monk shouldn't have known that. At the very least, not on that level of condescension.

I had slipped out of an uncomfortable shoe for an evening and now was trying to shove my swollen foot back into it and it wouldn't go.

He clicked from screen to screen, checking directories. "... It's gone," he said again, more to the screen than to me. "Not deleted. I can tell you that it wasn't deleted. It was moved somewhere, but I can't tell where."

I looked back at my files. The missing documents had been research into a synthetic pharmacological compound, ED – 01 – N, codenamed "Vitality." It sounded like a male enhancement drug. There had been several pages worth of animal trials and thirty identity-protected sheets of human trials, each with their own case number. There was a password-protected file that, once opened, would provide the name and social security number that corresponded to each case number. It had been a part of a long night of audits for me nearly a month ago, the files a red haze even to me. They'd had positive results in uterine cancer, it had been mentioned. Other test subjects had noted cognitive shifts, possibly a side effect? Who knew. The files itself didn't matter so much as the fact that they were gone. They had been in my hands, I had audited them personally, and now they were gone.

Nelson continued to click through screens of text, some of which made sense to me but most of it nonsense. It was the bios of the network, the programs running in the background on the Shane system. "There's something else gone too," he said, almost to himself.

I looked up.

"See here?" he pointed to a folder he had opened from deep in the directory. It was from the applied sciences subdirectory, and it was empty. "It's empty here, but click back," he did so, "and it says the folder has 368 files. The same was with your R&D files: gone but not gone. Not invisible, not hidden, and not deleted. There in all the ways the computer tracks and regulates but not there in practice."

"The files are in deep cover," I said under my breath.

"What?"

"Nothing." I straightened. "Can you tell me what the files were about?"

Several more clicks. "A specific sort of centrifuge? Maybe? If you trust the file directory."

I placed my hand on his shoulder. "Let me know if you find anything else. Only me, if you can."

He nodded.

CHAPTER NINETEEN

Maggie and I attended a Charlie Chaplin double feature at the Bijou the next week. I'd gotten the idea after hearing her go on about seeing RDJ (I was calling him that myself now) in the Chaplin biopic. They played *The Great Dictator* and *Gold Rush*... I didn't think too much of *Gold Rush* either way, but I couldn't help but watch *The Great Dictator* with undue attention.

Did you know that the film was controversial at the time for being anti-Hitler? This was in the time while Hitler was in power, but before the second World War. There's so much of our history we've just... erased. Nobody would say now that there was pro-Nazi sentiment in the US prior to World War II, but it was there and prominent. But it has been whitewashed from history. America was in its own version of deep cover, inventing a new history for itself as it went along and insisting upon the fictional version as truth. History, Shane, Simon Monk: all of us under deep cover, hiding aspects of ourselves.

We went out for dinner afterward at a quaint little bistro that took cash only. The kitchen was in the middle of the dining room and the entire restaurant was filled with flavorful steam that permeated everything. They made this succulent lamb medallion that broke apart like butter the second you touched it with your fork... I tell you, there was nothing like it. It was the first time I had eaten something of my own choosing with my own tongue in twenty months, and it was like giving a dry man water: it filled me completely, made me whole and happy.

I walked her home again and again we kissed on her front stoop. It was neither her kissing me nor me kissing her this time, but rather something that happened naturally, like two halves coming together to make a whole. It was long and wet and slow and hungry, our lips still savory from the meal. Her perfume was on me and all around me; her hair was in my eyes and my mind and everywhere. After an eternity that felt too short, our lips parted, and a smile crept over hers.

I was smiling too, I realized. "Goodnight," I said, that dumb grin on my lips.

She took me by the hand, firmly and gently, and led me inside instead.

CHAPTER TWENTY

It was a familiar setting, and yet not. Old and yet wholly new: me on a couch, my lips pressed to a beautiful woman. Her hands were on me and in my hair and around me. She pulled me by the collar back onto the couch atop her, her lips soft and forceful in a way I am convinced no other thing in nature could be.

"Simon..." she said in hushed whisper, and I flinched. I must have flinched, for she flinched.

As I said: familiar, yet wholly new. Every touch was intensified, every caress, every graze. It had been too long since I had had an unexpected experience... even when I was the prey as I'd played for Lydia Carter, I was really the one behind it all. I had had no idea this was coming, and the spontaneity of it made my heart race and my blood pump in a way it hadn't in years.

I also couldn't remember the last time I had been in this position with someone I cared for.

The realization made me wince again.

"Simon—"

With the realization came anxiety. There's a reason American's hide the unfortunate political leanings of the past; through today's lens, it would make them think of themselves differently. It was the same with Shane when one came down to it: they hid what they did not want people to see, perceptions they did not want made public.

And what about Maggie? Would she have taken me by the hand and led me into her home and kissed me on the neck (and now the ear, oh my) if she knew some of the things I'd done? I'd love to be able to tell you that bringing a cougar to climax was the worst of my deeds, but we both know it is not. In my experience, one does not even enter the trade of giving up one's identity unless one is ashamed of something they've done to begin with. When Maggie learned the truth, would she want to erase me? Would I become another faded pencil line on the paper of her soul, forever rubbed out and forgotten along with college boyfriends and other past mistakes? Would she have been here with me if I had not been Simon Monk?

"Simon—"

Her hands grasped at the clasp of my trousers and opened them, each digit hungry and wanting more and more of me. Just as before, my hand reached up and touched hers gently, but forcing it to stop.

"Simon?" She stopped moving and kissing me, able to see me now for the first time. Her head jolted back and her voice took on a wet tonality. "Simon, why are you crying?"

My hand went to my cheek: I was. I hadn't realized it, but I had been crying. Not openly weeping, but there was a steady stream of tears down my face. "I'm sorry," I said. I buttoned my trousers reflexively. "Maggie, I'm so sorry."

I had never said those words before, to anyone.

Her touch was gentle on my shoulder. When she spoke, she said, "It's alright, Simon." She said it with certainty, with a level of conviction that I had never had toward anything... anything, perhaps, save her. It was not that she couldn't conceive of what it might be and was ignorant of the possibilities: she weighed the possibilities and decided that whatever they were, it was okay. Her faith was something I did not deserve, that Simon Monk could never deserve.

And so I told her.

CHAPTER 20A

Simon took a long sip of his tea as the man across from him stared blankly.

"Well?" the man said finally, brushing his blond hair back from his eyes.

Simon looked up from his teacup, feigning ignorance. "Well, what?"

"What happened?"

Simon smiled. "A gentleman doesn't tell."

CHAPTER TWENTY X

"I'm a spy," Simon said, his hands clasped in a motion of prayer as they wiped the tears from his eyes. Moisture still dribbled from the cleft of his chin through the rough terrain of his five o'clock shadow.

A single syllable of a giggle erupted from Maggie Winter's lips. Had it not been for his tears, it would have been a full-fledged laugh. Even so the smile was in her eyes and she tried to fight it, tried to take it seriously... but it was so silly.

"I'm serious," he said again, his voice flat.

"Role play is a little much for the first time, don't you think?" She moved closer to him, but he shifted away. Her smile lessened slightly, and he hated to see it. He wanted to take it back, to laugh it off and take comfort in her lips and her touch and her body... But he couldn't. It had to be made clear. It had to be driven home.

"I manipulated myself into Shane as a means of industrial espionage, in order to get information for my employer."

Her smile was gone now, and she moved away from him. Not much, only a millimeter, but enough to send pangs through his heart. "Is this a joke? It's not funny if it's a joke."

He swallowed. "In order to get the information I needed on an upcoming merger --"

"Merger? What m--"

"I seduced Lydia Carter, Tyler's wife." He could not
look at her when he said this last.

She looked at him, then away, and then back again.
"Are you... What? How could... what? Who even does
that, what could you..." She got up off the couch.

"Maggie, please."

"Don't you dare. Don't you dare. Is this why I'm here,
is this why you're here, Mr. Monk? Did you need to get
into the accounting books so you thought you'd go about
it the fun way first? Is that how you get your rocks off?"

He swallowed. "Many years ago, I was in Niger. I was
working for Turkey at the time... it's not important. Someone had gone missing, and when I found him there were
two of them. Two men, the one I was looking for, and another." His accent slowly seeped in, adding a twang to the
end of certain words. Salt water tears were getting in his
mouth. "Those men... they changed me. It changed everything. Everything was different then... He and I went back
to Turkey and took a message back to my employers, but
these were not men easily trifled with --"

"*Why* are you telling me this?" she interjected, her
cheeks livid and hot. "Why do you think I *care*? Why
would you tell me any of this, Mr. Monk? What could
possibly be in this for you?"

He sucked in his lower lip and took a deep, shudder-
ing breath. "I couldn't be with you without you knowing
who I was," he said finally. He reached out and took her

cheek in his hand, and was surprised when she let him. "Not with you. Never, with you."

She looked at him, in the eyes, her cheeks still red with fury. After a moment she reached up and took his hand away from her cheek... but instead of forcing it away, she held it and kissed it, and knelt down in front of him finally. "That's a lot to take in."

"I know. I'm sorry... there's no easy way to say it."

She paused, for a very long time. "Is Lydia okay?"

He nodded. "We were not intimate. I... got the information I needed without taking it that far."

She nodded, bringing her hand up to wipe her face quickly, hoping he wouldn't see. After another long, tense silence... she laughed again, this time a full and complete laugh, not one stifled by poise or posturing. It took a minute, but he smiled. Her laugh made him smile, and he thought it was the loveliest sound he had ever heard. After a moment they kissed again, long but without hunger: it was a kiss of catharsis... another first for him in a long day of firsts, but for her as well.

"Well, Mr. Monk," she smirked at him. "Is that all now? Have you unburdened yourself?"

He looked at her pleadingly. "I'm sorry... my name is not Monk."

She made an exaggerated nod, as though she thought she should have expected that next. She put her hands against his biceps. "Well then, to whom do I have the pleasure?"

He smiled weakly. "Siaz."

She snorted again, releasing a long belly laugh that bubbled up from her and thrust her forward into his lap unintentionally. "I'm sorry, *now* you're kidding me. Simon Siaz? Your name is Simon Siaz?! As in, 'Simon Says touch your nose?'"

His eyes moistened again as she met his gaze through squinted, laughing eyes.

It took a moment to dawn on her, but when she did the laughter stopped. "Oh... oh, I see... Your name isn't Simon either, is it?"

"It is now," he said declaratively in his native accent for the first time in twenty months, and he brought his face to hers and kissed her.

CHAPTER TWENTY-ONE X

He kissed her with the sort of reckless abandon he hadn't allowed himself in years... perhaps ever. He held nothing back and kept nothing in, his hands cupping her face and then moving to her collarbone and then her shirt was gone, fluttering quickly through the air of her home until it landed softly against a chest. Her hair fell down over her shoulders like something out of a Sandro Botticelli, and for once in his adult life the only conflict he felt was whether he would rather gaze upon her forever or have her; if only he could have done both.

Once again she fumbled with the clasp of his pants, tugging the two halves apart... and once again, he faltered. "Maggie --"

She let out an exaggerated, exasperated, humored sigh, smiling at him. "What? Is there something else? Are you North Korean? Were you on the Manhattan Project?" She kissed him on the cheek.

"The men... there are cruel men in this world. Some of them I have worked for... some of them I no longer work for..."

She smiled. "I'm a big girl, and this isn't a comic book." She kissed him again, lightly, on the lips. "Nobody is going to come throw me off the Brooklyn Bridge."

"No, these men were not happy that I left, when I was in Niger... the man I was sent to stop, he helped me... but they were vicious men."

She took him by the ears. "Then I'll be gentle," she hummed laughingly.

"Maggie --"

At once, she understood. It all clicked into place, suddenly, and she nodded. Her face poised and sweet and serious, she leaned in and kissed him on the lips... the new best kiss of the newly christened Simon's life, and though he did not know it then, the best kiss he would ever have. The first kiss between a soul unburdened and another unfazed, each one seeing the other for what they truly were and accepting it, totally and without consequence or malice.

For a third time she reached for his middle, sliding her small hand between his skin and the fabric of his clothes. Her hand moved deftly and silently, up then down then up again, her lips pressed firmly to his the entire time. When her hand emerged again, she withdrew his penis.

It had been sliced vertically down the middle through four of its roughly eight inches, the two halves splaying in either direction like a dousing rod. The bulb was darkened and wrinkled. The foreskin had been wrapped around the half that stuck out to the right, giving the impression that the left half was a second, thinner member that splayed bare to the side due to bad plastic treatment. The foreskin, and indeed the skin of much of his groin, was noticeably lighter than the rest of him and did not move and twitch with the rest. The flesh that was colored 'correctly' was shrivelled and tight with scar tissue.

She broke off their kiss and pressed her cheek to his, regarding the part of him that lay limply in her hand. She moved it slowly, smoothly between her fingers, the right half between her thumb and forefinger as she led the foreskin over the bulb and back again, the left half cradled gently by her ring and forefinger.

Her cheek was hot and pleasant against his. They watched her actions together, each equally invested.

"How long has it been?" she asked quietly, without turning to look at him.

"It has been like this seven years."

"No, I mean, how long has it been since --"

"It has been seven years."

She nodded. "I'm sorry."

"No, I'm sorry." He winced. "I'm sorry after all this that I can't... I have pills, but they're at the house... and they're not much good. I hadn't expected."

She nodded, still manoeuvring his member slowly and carefully between her digits, then turned so that she could kiss him again as she did. When this kiss was done, she moved her mouth, moist and warm, to his chin and then his neck.

"What are..." he started, then caught himself somewhere between surprise and shame. "You can't."

She did not respond. Her mouth found her way to the right splay of his genitals and she cupped it gently along her tongue before taking it into her mouth almost to where the halves split, gently holding the left half all the while and keeping it safe. She moved it with her as she moved, down to exacting detail.

He winced once and tried faintly to object, then felt the muscles in his shoulders relax and refuse to stop her. She had taken him over. He was Pinocchio without his strings, lying prostrate before her power.

She cupped him gingerly as she moved, paying careful attention to every sound and motion he made, knowing then where to go and where not to go... and after what felt like forever, he felt something he had not felt in so long he had stopped believing it was a possibility, as he began to rise within the soft embrace of her lips. Blood filled him and expanded him, making him more a man than he had thought himself able in almost two Olympiads. She slowed as he grew, and as he thought she was finishing, she released him from her velvet tongue... then tenderly eased the left splay of his penis up so that it was in line with the right, lowering her head again until all of him was in her.

He tried again to object, but found he could not. Alarms and fireworks blared out the back of his skull and made it impossible to think. Pain mixed with ecstatic, revenant pleasure as she moved him within her and his vision went white around the corners, his every muscle going ridged and seizing with spasms of electric current.

He ejaculated, and the sound that came from him was ecstasy. His voice echoed off the walls and filled her home until it was bursting from the very floorboards, deep and full and in every cell of his being.

When he came back down to earth, she was at his side, her button nose stroking at the nape of his neck. He turned his head down and kissed her passionately. He was still cradled in the palm of her hand, glistening in the low light of her living room now. As he kissed her, she began to rock him again.

He smiled and chuckled. "Maggie... once was a miracle. I'm sorry --" But he stopped short, as his body made a liar of him.

She took his head in her hand and laid him back onto the couch until he was flat. She stood briefly, her breasts bare in the soft glow from her kitchen, and removed her underwear from under her dress. She lifted one leg and stepped over him, then again cupped him in her hands. She had become nimble at it now; there wasn't any hesitation. It was an instrument she picked up as though she had every night since time immortal.

He brought his hands to her thighs and slowly began to push her dress up. She stopped him in a mirror of the way he had her, her hands gentle on his.

"What?" he asked, his voice a whisper.

She smiled and laughed, a blush returning to her cheeks. "Promise you won't laugh?"

He nodded. "Never."

"... I don't like it when people look at me."

He did laugh, and she with him. He let her dress fall back around her and she gently brought him inside her, then leaned forward and kissed him as they rocked back and forth, her body clenching him as warmly and gently and lovingly as her hand had.

They arrived as one and she collapsed upon his chest with scant breath, where they remained for some time.

CHAPTER TWENTY-ONE

I awoke from a brief doze with her head on my chest, my legs spread along her couch, and I'd never felt more at ease with myself in my life. She was trailing her finger along the small nest of hair that existed between my nipples, not bored but aimless. It seemed like a reward in and of itself. I kissed her on the top of her head and felt her smile against me.

"So what are you investigating?" she asked, and I could tell by her tone it had been on her mind for some minutes. The question was casual though, with the air of someone who would accept any response even if that response was that I couldn't say.

"It's not like that."

"Then what's it like?"

"You're better not knowing."

She turned her head and gave me a look that told me exactly what she thought of any statement like that. "I'm an accountant. I could help."

"Too dangerous."

"And if I'm doing something wrong and not knowing it, I want to know."

I frowned, then shifted so that we were beside one another. I took several hard breaths, trying to find the right words. Lies were so much easier than the truth. "It's not a matter of doing something wrong, per se. Although there's certainly something going on. It's more..." I shifted again. She kissed me on the corner of my mouth, and it energized me, bringing my thoughts into clear focus. "There are epistemic shifts in the world, especially in the political world. Big events that change... everything. They upset the balance of power. The people paying me, they don't so much want to stop these shifts so much as be prepared for them."

"Who's paying you?"

Now it was my turn to give her a look.

"Sorry."

"It's okay. These shifts, sometimes they're unpredictable: like the stock market crash. But the more of them that happen, the better people get *at* predicting them. In the same way that we learned about the weather by first watching the weather, or how we developed profiles on serial killers by first looking at the profiles and patterns of existing serial killers. These patterns – these cultural shifts – have been mapped out for over a century now, and the people behind the people in charge of the world are finally getting good at predicting them."

She sat with that for a moment, then nodded slowly before lying back on me. Her eyes traced the patterns on her ceiling as though seeing it for the first time. "So... the people paying you, they think one of these big shifts in going to happen at Shane?"

I hemmed, bobbing my head back and forth. How to explain? "Something's coming. We're long past due, and the world seems to keep boiling over with no hint at stopping. Shane is one of three big players in a certain space that we think is going to make a big difference in the next few years. With that kind of growth comes money, and with that kind of money comes power: lobbyists, political partnering, campaign donations... Shane's interests become the world's interests... and if that's the case, it would be good to know what Shane's interests are ahead of time."

We were both silent then for a very, very long time. The two halves of me had returned, the man who now in some part belonged to Maggie Winter and the deep cover, returning from his evening of rest. I knew what to ask but didn't want to, even once I realized that she was all but waiting for the question. "Have you noticed anything strange, in your audits?"

I could feel her tongue moving about against the inside of her cheek as she contemplated. "No... well, yes. But not really."

I stopped and turned toward her. "What was it?"

She paused, pursing her lips. "I've been seeing a *lot* of money coming in from the Engineering department. A lot of money, easily a quarter of our income last year. I brought it up to Tyler twice and he said it was misrouted and that he would find out where the funds really came from – but for now I'm to just keep track of it so it can be properly allocated when he knows where it should have been coming from."

I mulled on that for a moment. "I don't get it."

"...We don't have an Engineering department, Simon."

CHAPTER TWENTY-TWO

Maggie loved watching Robert Downey Junior play real life journalists. So did I, honestly, but his were by no means my favorite portrayals. For me you had to go all the way back to 1976, when Dustin Hoffman and Robert Redford played Woodward and Bernstein... the simplicity of real investigation always struck me. It was never a mastermind stroking a cat felled by a dashing Scotsman – more often than not, it was something small and simple like it was in 1976: "Follow the money."

I got the keys to the hard files from Nelson, told him I was looking for my missing files. It was partially true, and that was what made him not question it. The files mattered, yes. There was something to the files, to ED – 01 – N, relating to that specific type of centrifuge and who knew what else, and lord only knew how important those things were... but they were symptoms. They were the fever that came with the virus that was going to kill you. I could spend the next twenty months digging through files and investigating targeting malware to try and find everything that Shane had been up to... but they were all of them symptoms.

The disease had been right in front of sweet Maggie

Winter the entire time, and it made my lip curl to think of her soft hands organizing the files that helped clean the filth that came through.

Follow the money. Shane doesn't have an engineering department.

It took me less than five hours to find what I'd spent the last twenty months searching for as Simon Monk. Twenty months as Simon Monk bested by one word from the most amazing woman Simon Siaz had ever met.

Animal trials and clinical trials and human trials and synthetic drugs and new centrifuges and god-only-knew what else all had one thing in common: they cost money. Lots, and lots of money. The type of money that made the cash I had spent making myself looking like a good management consultant or a competent stock advisor seem like pennies.

Shane is one of three big players in the space that are going to make a big difference in the next few years.

Tyler won't be home all night... he practically sleeps at the office getting ready for the merger.

Money like that didn't come from just anywhere, and certainly not without a heavy caveat attached. Shane had been paid billions hidden through a department that didn't exist to do research and development on behalf of the payee. That much money doesn't just buy goods and services: it buys stock. Lots of stock, carefully changing hands outside of the public eye as the engineering department kept the money coming in... as the stock was slowly being filtered out. It was my stock shift I'd used to trick Tyler, on a massive scale. On an astronomical scale.

The money had come from different places, all filtered

through engineering. OmegaGene and Crytech and Alpha Quadrant and Slipfire and private hands... all that money coming in and all that stock going out, no one the wiser that it was all filtering back to one place.

There are three big players in the space that are going to make a difference in the next few years.

It wasn't a merger... or if it was now, it hadn't started as one. It was the slowest takeover in history: thirty different small subsidiary companies contracting their work in exchange for money and stock options, the money staying with Shane, and the stock options all filtering back up to the parent company... until before Shane knows it, someone else holds that majority. Or close enough to a majority to render their management moot, and suddenly it's time to talk options. Does the current brass step down and let the void be filled with the people who took them over... or do they make a deal, becoming the largest of all the subsidiary companies in the process?

There are three big players in the space that are going to make a difference in the next few years.

CHAPTER TWENTY-THREE

I laid the folder down on the Joint Chief's desk. It was thick and meaty with pages, barely held together by the string that bound the manila-colored carrier together. I liked to make a show of it.

"That's all of it?" he said. His voice was high pitched and belied his sagging jowls. I wasn't sure how such a face could have even made such a voice.

I nodded.

He strummed his thumb down along the side. "I don't need to tell you that this stays between us."

"I've been paid, sir." It was the only acceptable answer to anything he said, ever.

"Thank you, Mr. Siaz. I have your next assignment." He held out a folder like the one I had handed him, but much thinner. I must have paused for a moment because he looked at me, but I snatched it an instant later. "Thank you, Mr. Siaz."

"Thank you, sir."

There is a part of me, a part that's still a spoiler, that would have loved to be a fly on the wall of that office when he opened the manila folder and realized that every one of those two hundred pages had been blank.

CHAPTER 23A

Simon sat with his arm bent back over the mesh chair he'd been sitting in for over an hour, sipping his second cup of coffee. It had gotten cold twice he had been talking so much, and the waitress had been kind enough to heat it with fresh pots again and again. The Arizona sun was bright in the sky and warm on his face as cars and children passed him by.

The man across from him with long blond hair and a stubbly goatee wore a tight black shirt, his arms crossed in front of it. He looked grim and thoughtful, but not unpleasant. The muscles in his arms caught deep shadows in the sunlight. "That's it then?" he asked, nodding respectfully.

Simon nodded, smiling. "Yes, Victor, that's it."

Victor un-tucked his hands and laid one on the manila folder in front of him. "And these are all the files?"

"Eighty-Six fairly incriminating pages, along with two *very* incriminating ones. It wasn't hard once I knew what to look for... I'm sorry I couldn't get more, but once things start going missing... people start looking."

Victor nodded. "You told the Joint Chief there were two hundred."

"Like I said, I like to make a show."

He nodded again. "This is too big to hide."

"I know."

"You're not going to be able to play triple agent anymore."

"I know." He looked across the street at a trim woman in a dress blazer and the most perfect dirty-blonde hair he had ever seen looking at travel brochures from a spinning rack. "And I'm fine with that, honestly. I've got some money tucked away... and good friends." He smiled when he said the last, throwing Victor a wink.

Victor touched the folder again, gently, as though afraid to. "... And you're sure?"

Simon met his eye. "The hint is in the name. The money came through the engineering department. There is no engineering department at Shane. Of the two companies that would have the interest and the resources to buy out Shane... I'd bet anything that the money came from Engen."

Victor let out a long sigh, gazing out over the crowd himself and finally coming to rest on a young brunette girl that was eyeing the tag on an orange dress that suited the day well. He decided immediately that he would buy it for her; her smile had a way of making him smile, and that was something he needed desperately at the moment.

"All's well that ends well?"

"One of the most clandestine organizations on the globe has acquired its only major competition for use as a public face. I'm not sure what you call ending well."

"Nobody hurt."

"Yet."

"Nobody dead."

"Yet."

"You can be a real downer, you know that?"

The blonde made her way across the street during a gap in traffic, then finally came over to their table. Victor forced a smile. "You must be Maggie. I've heard... a lot about you."

She shot Simon a look.

Simon extended a hand to Victor. "We square?"

Victor raised an eyebrow. "When have we not been square?"

Pause. "For Turkey."

Victor took his hand and shook it stiffly. "We've always been square for Turkey."

"Never," Simon said, clasping Victor's hand with both of his for a moment before reluctantly letting him go. He placed a hand gently on Maggie's back, and both of them started to walk away. "Take care of yourself, Victor. Live well."

Victor smiled as he got up. "I will!"

Smirking, Simon turned around in the middle of the empty street and waved his finger chidingly. "I didn't say Simon Says."

End.

ENGEN TIMELINE

With over twenty novels spread over three different series by many different authors, the Engen Universe of titles is growing every day and into genres we couldn't have imagined! From the original ten book *Black Womb* thriller series, its crime novel sequel series *Xander Drew*, our flagship adventure title *Infinity*, or single-novels like *Jacobi Street* or *light | dark,* there's something in the Engen Universe for everyone with more books by more authors on the way soon!

...But how do the events relate to one another, chronologically? While some astute readers have guessed at the potential timeline (some accurately, some not), we're going to finally set the question of the Engen Timeline to rest.

Turn the page for an up-to-date guide of the ever-widening world of Engen, featuring the works of Ellen Curtis, Andrea Hackett, Sarah Thompson, Jay Paulin, and Matthew LeDrew!

In the 10 Years Prior Black September

"Reptilia" by Matthew LeDrew
published in *light | dark*.
Danger descends on a small secluded town
in the form of a deadly virus with fantastic
and terrible side-effects. Can a small group of
doctors escape alive?

Compendium by Ellen Curtis
Three short stories forming the basis for the
Engen Universe's ties to suspense, genetic
engeneering, and the supernatural. Features
the stories "The Tourniquet Revival," "Falling
into Fire" and "At Midnight, the Dawn."

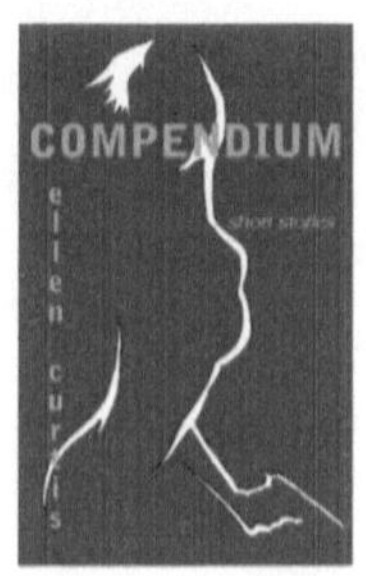

"The Theogony" by Matthew LeDrew
published in *light | dark*.
A tale of young Theo Flaherty of the *Infinity*
series and his time admitted against his will to
the Black Springs hospital, where he learns to
paint, and seeks out his father.

Black September

"Revving Engen" by Matthew LeDrew
published in *light | dark*.
A direct lead-in to both *Infinity* and *Black
Womb*, Tasha travels to Coral Beach, Maine on
a hot tip about a recently discovered young
man with incredible abilities.

Infinity by Ellen Curtis & Matthew LeDrew
Faced with a destiny he's uncertain of, the enigmatic Victor must bring together four unique people with very special abilities… or face the tasks ahead alone. Guaranteed to excite!

Black Womb by Matthew LeDrew
Fifteen years ago, something happened in Coral Beach, Maine that resulted in the present death of a seventeen-year-old boy. Now four high-school students must try to solve the mystery… before the killer picks them off.

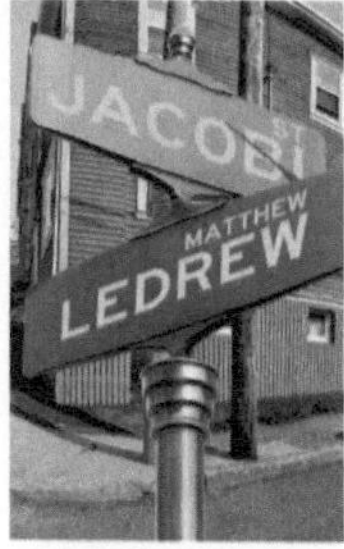

Jacobi Street by Matthew LeDrew
When a mysterious painting shows up at an art gallery he works at, Bob must work with Eddie and Sloan to track down its sinister origins and convince the people living on Jacobi Street of them, before its too late!

Transformations in Pain by Matthew LeDrew
When two girls are assaulted and one is hospitalized, the residents of Coral Beach must put their shared tragedies behind them and stop the man responsible, as well as unlock the secrets behind the true nature of the Womb…

Year One: October

Smoke and Mirrors by Matthew LeDrew
The approaching trial of Genblade brings
closure to the people of Coral Beach, until
people start showing up dead in the same
manner they did when he was at large.

"Scarlett" by Andrea Hackett
published in *light|dark*.
Introducing Scarlett, the slightly damaged
hunter on a mission to save others from the
monsters from her past.

The Tourniquet Reprisal by Curtis & LeDrew
A man lives in Atlanta, Georgia that people
don't talk about, but everyone knows he's
there. He arrived a year ago and turned a
gaggle of uneducated youth into something
new, something to fear.

Roulette by Matthew LeDrew
As the teen suicide rate in Coral Beach starts
to climb astronomically fast, Xander travels
to Los Angeles to fight his most terrifying
adversary yet… and learns that the only thing
worse than looking for release… is finding it.

Year One: November

Exodus of Angels by Curtis & LeDrew
Victor's enigmatic past is illuminated when Jaycee accompanies him to visit a new friend in the paliative care ward of the Black Springs hospital, where Theo also happens to be searching for a cure for Leigh.

Ghosts of the Past by Matthew LeDrew
Coral Beach faces its most awesome threat when one of Engen's past mistakes is unleashed upon the unsuspecting populous. Friends and enemies unite to fight a common enemy… but will even that be enough?

Touch Your Nose by Matthew LeDrew
Simon Monk must infiltrate the San Fransico branch of Shane Industries, a massive company with deep ties to the Engen Universe. Where do his true loyalties lie? And can he get out without causing harm?

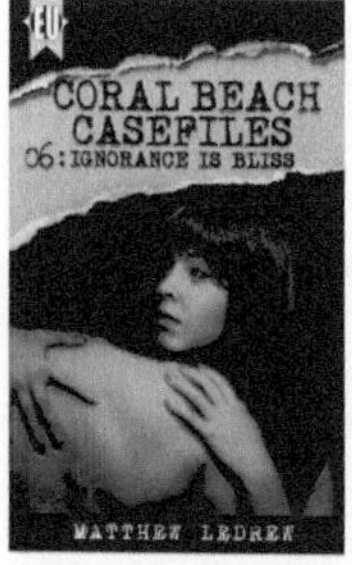

Ignorance is Bliss by Matthew LeDrew
After being set through the ringer one too many times, Xander decides that his life with Julie needs a little more attention… which is bad news because a new villain has come to town with his sights set on Adam Genblade.

"Gristle While You Work" by Jay Paulin
published in *light|dark*.
A short story centering around the rise of a
new, and possibly cannibalistic, serial killer in
the Engen Universe.

Becoming by Matthew LeDrew
For months Xander Drew has been doing his
level best to keep the streets of Coral Beach
clean, which means it's time for the forces of
darkness to strike back… all at once.

Inner Child by Matthew LeDrew
Julie is hospitalized with life-threatening
wounds to both body and soul. But the
real threat comes from the hospital walls
themselves, as a demonic presence makes itself
known to Xander and his friends.

End of Year One

Gang War by Matthew LeDrew
The Tees, a homicidal gang of evil men, has
finally been taken down by Xander Drew. But
his victory is short lived, as retired Tees are
mysteriously killed. With a town of suspects,
anyone can be the culprit… including one of
their own.

Chains by Matthew LeDrew
Sociopath Derek Smith has been freed from prison and is praying on the weak; and none are weaker than August Styles: a pregnant girl with Down Syndrome who has run away from home.

"Omega" by Ellen Curtis
published in *light|dark*.
A sinister division of Engen begins a series of experiments on pregnant women in a fashion eerily similar to those that created the original Black Womb project.

The Long Road by Matthew LeDrew
Xander meets the American people — and realizes that the world is harsh and wicked, but can also be soft and gentle, even loving. Xander Drew comes of age on the road, and sets his new direction.

Year Two

Cinders by Matthew LeDrew
Detective Horton enters a violent and dangerous world he didn't know existed beneath the veneer of order and structure that he has based his entire deductive method around.

Sinister Intent by Matthew LeDrew
One of the killers Detective Horton could not catch has resurfaced: a serial killer who flaunts his sinister intent in front of the Los Angeles Police Department, making it so that no one is safe.

Faith by Matthew LeDrew
Xander's mysterious and troublesome past returns to haunt him on the streets of Los Angeles; a place where even more people can get caught in the crossfire of the games of death and deceit that makes up his life.

Flickers in the Night by Matthew LeDrew
Lisa Rowdan is hunted by her haunting -- and powerful -- ex-boyfriend Ryan through a lonely city street. Can she escape him?
One of over twenty great sprine-tingling short stories!

Family Values by Matthew LeDrew
Xander and his new friends Crowley, Lisa, and Tim investigate a series of kidnappings and murders that stretch back decades, all of which have the same similar twist: victims being found after years of being missing.

ABOUT THE AUTHOR

Matthew LeDrew holds an Honours Degree in English from the Memorial University of Newfoundland with a minor in Anthropology, and studied Journalism at College of the North Atlantic in Stephenville, Newfoundland. He was honoured to be a jury member of the 2018 NLBA awards.

He has written twenty novels for Engen Books: the ten book *Coral Beach Casefiles* series, *The Long Road, Cinders, Sinister Intent, Faith, Family Values, Jacobi Street, Touch Your Nose, Infinity, The Tourniquet Reprisal, and Exodus of Angels* the latter three of which with co-author Ellen Curtis.

He lives in St. Johns, Newfoundland.